Penguin Modern Classics
On the Marble Cliffs

Ernst Jünger was born at Heidelberg in 1895. He ran
away from school to enlist in the Foreign Legion (see
Afrikanische Spiele, translated as *African Diversions*);
and in 1914 he volunteered, was commissioned, often
wounded, and highly decorated for his leadership of
storm troops. His war experience is recorded in *In
Stahlgewittern* (*The Storm of Steel*), of which there are
many revised editions, *Der Kampf als inneres Erlebnis*,
Das Wäldchen 125 (*Copse 125*), and *Feuer und Blut*. It is
recorded not as an aberration but as a revelation. The
resulting ideal of self-transcendence he developed into a
totalitarian doctrine of society in *Die Totale
Mobilmachung* (1931) and *Der Arbeiter* (1932). Although
the Nazis often quoted him, he remained critical of them,
and his next two novels sought a more individual
meaning in suffering and sacrifice.
On the Marble Cliffs (1939) is an allegorical novel, and in
this and *Heliopolis* (1944) and *The Glass Bees* (1957) he
traces confusing conflicts between principles of anarchy
and despotism, violence and contemplation. Striking
passages of nature description found in these books (he
had studied zoology at Leipzig and Naples) also
distinguish many of his fine essays and travel books.

Ernst Jünger

On the Marble Cliffs

Translated from the German
by Stuart Hood

Penguin Books

Penguin Books Ltd, Harmondsworth,
Middlesex, England
Penguin Books, 40 West 23rd Street,
New York, New York 10010, U.S.A.
Penguin Books Australia Ltd, Ringwood,
Victoria, Australia
Penguin Books Canada Limited, 2801 John Street,
Markham, Ontario, Canada L3R 1B4
Penguin Books (N.Z.) Ltd, 182–190 Wairau Road,
Auckland 10, New Zealand

Auf den Marmorklippen first published in Germany by
Ernst Klett Verlag 1939
This translation first published in Great Britain by
John Lehmann 1947
This translation first published in the United States of America by
New Directions Publishing Corp. 1948
Published in Penguin Books 1970
Reprinted 1983

Printed in the United States of America by
R. R. Donnelley & Sons Company, Harrisonburg, Virginia
Set in Linotype Times

Translator's Note

Since Ernst Jünger's *Auf den Marmorklippen* was first published in Hamburg in 1939, it is not surprising to find that the author indulges in a certain amount of mystification in his description of how a tyrant came to power. What is a matter for astonishment is that the disguises under which certain of the characters appear are so transparent. There are episodes, too – notably the excursion to Köppels-Bleek – which are so unequivocal that one cannot but be amazed. It is the author's contention, however, that the book is more than a parable of the rise of Nazism; it is, he asserts, a study of the essential nature of tyranny, and as such applicable to any age and to any totalitarian state.

In order to stress the universal application of his *In Tyrannos*, Jünger has taken certain liberties with time and place. The landscape round the Marble Cliffs contains elements from the Bodensee, South America and Italy. The time of the action is as indeterminate as the location of the Marina or Alta Plana. As in a dream, there is no certain boundary between past, present and future; the author can and does move in time at will.

Beyond these few aids to comprehension of the book it is not the duty of the translator to go. He must leave it to the reader to decide whether the manner of Braquemart's death – by biting a capsule of poison – is to be classed as coincidence or whether, as the author would have it, as something akin to prophecy.

S. C. H.

Introduction

Ernst Jünger's *In Stahlgewittern* (*The Storm of Steel*) appeared in 1920 and brought him immediate fame. It remains the most remarkable piece of *writing* to come out of the First World War. I emphasize 'writing'. Guy Chapman's *Passionate Prodigality* is a more penetrating, unbroken act of human perception; the political reach of Barbusse's *Le Feu* is greater. But Ernst Jünger came nearer than any other writer, nearer even than the poets, to forcing language into the mould of total war. This is in part a matter of technique: the lapidary sentences, so different from the sinuous hesitance of normal German literary and philosophic prose, the violent similes, the play of graphic, uncontrolled turbulence against abstraction. In part it stems from Jünger's resolve to make the job of writing a counterpart to that of combat. War and his personal virtuosity at the game – seven times wounded, platoon leader Jünger received Germany's highest military award in September 1918 – became the visionary core, the final touchstone, of the entirety of Jünger's work. The chaotic hell of the Somme and Langemarck grew into more than a searing memory or an instance of life turned lunatic. The fire-storm of the big guns, the moon-landscape of craters and flares, the somnambular frenzies of hand-to-hand fighting, seemed to Jünger to compact certain essential truths and mysteries in man. After such battle there could be no peace, only an armistice. To write essays, poems or novels as if language itself had not passed through barbed wire and poisoned air, looked to Jünger like romantic evasion, like a bourgeois tactic at a time when the moorings of bourgeois civilization had been fatally loosed. Though inextricably a part of violence, language was nevertheless the last zone of assured survival.

In March 1943, in occupied Paris, Captain Jünger noted in his diary: 'When all buildings shall be destroyed, language will none the less persist. It will be a magic castle with towers and battlements, with primeval vaults and passageways which none will ever search out. There, in deep galleries, *oubliettes* and mine-shafts it will be possible to find habitation and be lost to the world. Today that thought consoles me.'

The notion of language as an absolute, as the locus of ultimate reality and survival, is one of the two mainsprings of Jünger's art. The other is the pursuit of the biological sciences. Beginning almost immediately after 1919, Jünger turned to the study of botany, of ichthyology and entomology. His acquaintance with crustaceans, lepidoptera, with endless varieties of coleoptera, gastropod molluscs and arachnids goes far beyond the amateur. Above all, Jünger is a passionate botanizer. There are few pages in his diaries and travel books, fewer still in his two allegoric fictions, on which we do not find some exact glimpse of plant-life. Victoria Regia blooms in the hot, battle-scarred marshes; the red woodland orchid 'with the pale tip to the petals' shimmers in the dusk; a few days after learning of the death of his only son on the Italian front, Jünger observes the fibrous, yellow-green frond of blossoms on the hazel bush outside his window. Many values relate to this taxonomic compulsion. Like André Gide, Jünger regards zoology and botany as a school for precise feeling; the eye of the beetle-hunter, of the collector of orchidaceae becomes as penetrating and scrupulous as that of the sniper. Having immersed himself in the wasteful destruction of men, Jünger finds a guarantor of reality in the tenacity and profusion of organic life. That low perennial herb *Convalaria majalis*, the lily of the valley, will blow cool and luminous when our concrete bunkers are dust. But plant morphology, the comparative study and classification of flora, has an even deeper meaning. Linnaeus is Ernst Jünger's tutelary spirit. Like Goethe, Jünger deems the classification of floral species to be a supreme metaphor of reason, of the secret concord between the image of order in the human soul and the realities of significant relations in

8

nature. By assembling the great *Hortus Plantarum Mundi,* man comes as near as is possible to the lost Garden of creation. Moreover to recognise plants by their sporophylls, as Linnaeus did, is to 'read' an alphabet or cypher of life more ancient, more universal than any human idiom. In the tendril of the vine, in the hieroglyphs on the wings of the tiger-moth, the logic of creation is writ deep. The classic artist is one who can make his individual speech or form similarly suggestive of a hidden unity, of a total design of truth.

Jünger completed the manuscript of *On the Marble Cliffs* on 12 August 1939. A summer of exceptional radiance was drawing to a close. By the spring of 1940, some thirty-five thousand copies of *Auf den Marmorklippen* were in circulation. After that the authorities stopped further printings, but the book was not harried methodically, let alone pulped or burned as were many others. Reissued after the author's 'amnesty' in 1948 (Jünger had refused to appear before a German 'de-Nazification' tribunal), the novel had, twenty years later, passed the hundred-thousand mark.

Home from a long war, the narrator and his brother Otho (they are brethren both in the flesh and in a fraternity of elect spirits) settle in a hermitage carved into a spur of the marble cliffs. Below them stretches the Marina, a beauteous lake bordered by a land of ancient cities, sanctuaries and vineyards. The two warrior-sages seek to spend their lives in studying botany and in contemplation. In the chalice of the blue-starred gentian might lodge the inner penetralium, the secret towards which all magic, trance, alchemy and cabala direct their seemingly disparate but ultimately conjoined striving. In the Rue-Garden Hermitage dwell Erio, the elf-child of a brief erotic encounter which the narrator had in war time, and his grandmother, the earth-witch Lampusa. A brood of lance-head vipers weave their golden coils, whistling round about the hermitage. The Marina is shadowed by black forests. Here rules the Head Ranger, a cunning, savage tyrant. His horde of thugs and killers are the Mauretanians; their raids and propaganda are undermining the ancient modes of cultured life in the land of Marina. Between Marina and Mauretania lies the Campagna, an intermediary terrain of steppes and rough pasture. It is inhabited by archaic, hospitable peoples and Belovar, their wild patriarch.

On the Marble Cliffs recounts the doom of this unstable triad. The herdsmen of the Campagna are deserting their pastoral deities; strange enervations fester in the Marina. One day, probing into the Mauretanian forest, the brothers come upon the Flayer's Copse:

> Over the dark door on the gable-end a skull was nailed fast, showing its teeth and seeming to invite entry with its grin. Like a jewel in its chain, it was the central link of a narrow gable frieze which appeared to be formed of brown spiders. Suddenly we guessed that it was fashioned of human hands fastened to the wall. So clearly did we see this that we picked out the little peg driven through the palm of each one.
>
> On the trees, too, which ringed the clearing, bleached the death's-heads . . .
>
> . . . At the same time there bore down upon the wind a clinging heavy and sweet smell of corruption which made us shiver to the marrow of our bones. Within us we felt the melody of life touch its darkest and deepest chord.

When the *Oberförster* unleashes his attack, the narrator joins a troop of farmers and peasants to do desperate battle. The actual mêlée is fought mainly between Belovar's noble greyhounds and the giant mastiffs of the Mauretanians. Pursued by Chiffon Rouge, the Ranger's favourite killer-bloodhound, the narrator flees down the cliffs to the hermitage. Summoned by Erio, the vipers interpose a barrier of flame and venom between the brothers and the murdering pack. The realm of the Marina goes under in an apocalypse of fire, blood and crashing masonry. Otho and the narrator board a vessel, mysteriously ready for them, and escape to a far shore. There, in the mountain fastness of Alta Plana, the halls of Ansgar bide their festive coming.

Admirers of Ernst Jünger, apologists for the right-wing élitism and nationalist mystique he advocated in the

1920s and 30s, have hailed *Auf den Marmorklippen* as anti-Nazi. It has been widely asserted that this arcane fable is the only major act of resistance, of inner sabotage, carried out by German literature under Hitler. Jünger himself has been more circumspect, and rightly so. The depiction of the Head Ranger and his Mauretanian gangs is obviously directed against Nazism. The very name 'Chiffon Rouge' evokes the blood-red banners which went before the marching SS. Jünger's narrative of the processes of menace and subterranean blackmail whereby the forest horde insinuates itself into the daily lives and even the dreams of Marina and the Campagna, is a first-class piece of political observation and satire. His account of the visit to the hermitage of Braquemart and the young Prince of Sunmyra is both acute and prophetic. In this scene, probably the subtlest in the book, the impotence of traditional elements in German society, the surrender to opportunism or elegant despair of those forces that might have challenged Hitler, are deeply etched. But no scheme of straightforward political allegory or subversion fits. Even the bestial image of the Flayer's Copse is less trenchant or unambiguous than might appear. The analogy with the concentration camps about which Jünger had heard and intimated a good deal as early as 1939, but against which he never raised a public cry, is evident and graphic. But the dwarf who plies his butcher's craft in the clearing of Köppels-Bleek belongs less to the macabre repertoire of National Socialism than he does to the world of Wagner's Mime or to the malignant trolls of Scandinavian saga. And how betrayingly bathetic, how devoid of genuine fury is the reference to the 'melody of life' with which the passage closes. Belovar can be equated with no recognizable contemporary political stance. His roistering homestead, his patriarchal fierceness, suggest a version of pastoral as Teutonic, as deep-rooted in the ideal of *Blut und Boden* as were the Nordic fantasies of Rosenberg.

What is one to make of the end of the fable? For all its manifest terror, the destruction of the Marina elicits from Otho and the narrator a highly ambivalent response. The

11

spectacle of ruin seems to them filled with a strange beauty and somehow justified or, at least, sanctified by doom. (Meditating on the plot against Hitler in July 1944, which he had refused to join, Jünger wondered whether a nation ought, by mere accident and artifice of individual deeds, to escape its tragic destiny.) Though fleeing for their lives, the elect brethren acquiesce, at a disturbingly central level, in the barbaric triumph of the Mauretanians:

> No house is built, no plan laid, of which decay is not the corner-stone, and what lives eternally in us does not lie in our works. This we perceived in the flames, and yet there was joy in their radiance. . . . Our hearts felt that the fires in the sky had begun to lose something of their balefulness; they were mingled with the red of dawn.

For the lordly few there is sanctuary in Alta Plana. How, except by gross simplification, can one read this Nietzschean, hieratic close as an attack on Hitlerism, let alone a call to active resistance? Though he writes from an obvious propagandistic bias, Helmut Kaiser, one of Jünger's East German critics, is scarcely wrong when he characterizes the 'message' of *On the Marble Cliffs* as one of haughty, almost vindictive despair. The existence of the Marina is doomed not only because the evil powers of the forest are so great and ruthless. The humanistic values of life in the vineyards and comely cities are not worth preserving. They are sapped by bourgeois decay. Let Heraclitean fire purge all.

The true consistency of Jünger's parable is personal. The vipers that guard the narrator are immediately cognate to the Orphic and literal snakes (group *Ophidia*, order *Squamata*) which obsess Jünger's fantasies and with which his meticulously recorded dreams are replete. Brother Otho stands for Friedrich Georg Jünger, himself a poet and naturalist. Father Lampros has his recognizable model in the Jünger circle. Above all, the portrait of the narrator is insistently autobiographical. He has Jünger's port and style of vision. He too dwells among serpents, flowers and ancient, stately things. He is a soldier who makes of battle

12

a *rite de passage* into the hidden places of the spirit. His inward home is the *Burgunderland*, a partly historical, partly emblematic amalgam of French and German latinity which fascinates Jünger as it did Stefan George and Ernst Robert Curtius. At the nadir of the Reich, Jünger still joined other Knights of the Order of *Pour le mérite* in commemorative ceremonies in Berlin. Similarly, the warrior-dreamers of the *Marmorklippen* intimate the survival, beyond all present disaster, of an occult chivalry. At many points, it is difficult to distinguish between allegory and personal memoir. In July 1943, for example, Jünger's diary alludes to a 'mysterious' visit from Heinrich von Trott, a visit which presumably took place in 1938 or 1939 and had some relation to clandestine action against Hitler; in the dialogue with Braquemart and the young Prince, that visit is already recorded.

Ernst Jünger's fairy-tale is as cold and inert as its haunting title. Though composed of the short sentences which are characteristic of his manner, it achieves the laboured solemnity of a slow-motion film. No shaft of humour dents its burnished panoply. The tale is brimful of pain and violence. Yet they are seen in a distancing light. The battle of the great hounds is one of the cruellest set-pieces in modern fantasy. The narrator himself compares the scene with the pit of hell. Nevertheless, the dominant note is one of unreality, of ceremonious stillness. It is as if all the maddened, wildly moving shapes were transfixed in the heavy cadence of a dream. Where have we seen that murderous chase before, that ornate blaze of spears and torches in a night-forest? In the paintings of Uccello. Uccello is an arresting painter; but he is also a minor master, or one whose brilliant work is marginal to the main energies of Renaissance art. Eroded by sentimentality and middle-class taste, his hard enamelling, his static violence, re-appear in the Pre-Raphaelites. Jünger's eye is strikingly akin to that of Millais and Rossetti. Both aesthetics register the same minute details of flora and fauna, the same tints of precious stones and woven silk. Jünger's journals record a mania for

13

curiosa, for eighteenth-century erotica, for the florid and gilt bric-à-brac of European and oriental mundanity. He shares with painters and poets of the *fin-de-siècle* an amateurist interest in sadism. On the Paris quais, Captain Jünger pores over dusty chronicles of chastisement and execution. Cannibalism haunts his imagination and he notes, with a curator's precision, what evidence there is of its re-emergence on the Russian front and in the starving prison camps.

The inspirers of Jünger's sensibility are French rather than German. It is the post-symbolist and decadent movements in French literature that he draws on most directly: Huysmans, Léon Bloy, Octave Mirbeau, whose *Jardin des supplices* conjoins in its very title two of Jünger's abiding interests. In its terrible detachment, Jünger's *Strahlungen*, the record of his years in occupied Paris and of his conducted tour on the Caucasian front, is reminiscent of some of the Goncourt journals, particularly for 1870–71. In both cases the ultimate strategy is one of experience mastered by elegance. Whether he is noting the purchase of a rare engraving or the massacre of Jews, Jünger maintains a fastidious, quietly observant discipline of feeling. Watching a raid on the Renault works in March 1942, the chevalier of the marble cliffs comments that several hundred are reported slain and over a thousand gravely hurt: 'but seen from my quarter, the affair looked rather like stage-lighting in a shadow-theatre'. This is the focus of the dandy. I mean the word in its strong, *condottiero* sense, as comprehending asceticism and cool courage. The dandy confronts the sum of life but keeps it at gauntlet's length. Like his counterparts in the dramas of Montherlant, there is one temptation only which Jünger finds it really difficult to resist: *die Versuchung zur Menschenverachtung,* the temptation to despise human beings. Now I suspect that this attitude is more current among highly cultured men than one supposes. But Jünger makes a virtue of what is, essentially, a grave defect of consciousness, an atrophy at the vital centre.

14

A 'twentieth-century classic'? Perhaps so. But in an almost mathematical sense. *On the Marble Cliffs* is a theorem of limitation. It enacts the precise incommensurability between a certain cast of abstract humanism or high civilization and the realities of modern terror. In its ritual tranquillity, in its candid suggestion that flight into archaic utopia (the domain of privacy, of aesthetic and antiquarian cultivation) is the only way out, Jünger's legend embodies a tragic failure of nerve. Otho and his brother are custodians of ruin, as they are herbalists. Their powers of effective response are withered at the root. Jünger professes to have spent a lifetime in combat against nihilism; the spectre of nihilism haunts his post-war rhetoric. Yet there is in his own outlook – physically and psychologically implicated in the violent fabric of history as his personal career has doubtless been – a profound nihilism. Reading his work, one feels what Emily Dickinson termed 'a zero at the bone'.

The incapacity to feel lest feeling grow corrupt and banal is perhaps the paralysing dilemma of a classic, necessarily élitist culture. *Auf den Marmorklippen* has importance as a statement of this dilemma. The nocturnal word which Jünger himself applies to this condition is *tristia*. Through it blow the coldest winds from Limbo. Robbed of his only child, seeing Germany collapse into hideous abjection, Ernst Jünger attends a final, absurd meeting of local Nazi officials. He watches Hitler's thugs scheming their last act of murder or getting ready to scurry for cover. Yet no cry, no leap of rage escapes him. He notes in his diary: 'I lack the capacity for hatred.' There have been too many moments in our savage time when the absence of hatred is the same as the absence of love.

George Steiner, 1969

1

You all know the wild grief that besets us when we remember times of happiness. How far beyond recall they are, and we are severed from them by something more pitiless than leagues and miles. In the afterlight, too, the images stand out more enticing than before; we think of them as we do of the body of a dead loved one who rests deep in the earth, and who now in his enhanced and spiritual splendour is like a mirage of the desert before which we must tremble. And constantly in our thirst-haunted dreams we grope for the past in its every detail, in its every line and fold. Then it cannot but seem to us as if we had not had our fill of love and life; yet no regret brings back what has been let slip. Would that this mood might be a lesson to us for each moment of our happiness.

Sweeter still becomes the memory of our years by moon and sun when their end has been in the abyss of fear. Only then do we realise that for us mortals even this is great good-fortune – to live our lives in our little communities under a peaceful roof, with pleasing discourse and with loving greeting at morning and at night. Alas! always too late do we grasp that, if it offered no more than this, our horn of plenty brimmed with riches.

So it is that I think back to the times when we lived on the Great Marina – it is memory alone that evokes their charm. In those times, I will confess, it seemed to me that many cares and many troubles darkened our days, and, above all, we were on our guard against the Chief Ranger. So, although bound by no vow, we lived with a certain austerity and in homely garb. But twice a year we gave a glimpse of the brilliance of its red inner lining – once in the spring and once in the autumn.

In the autumn we feasted like sages and did honour to the exquisite wines in which the southern slopes of the Marina abound. When in the vineyards between red foliage and dark grape clusters we caught the jocund calls of the vintagers, when in the little towns and villages the wine-presses began to creak, and the odour of the pressed grape skins drew its heady veils round the farms, we would go down to the innkeepers, coopers and wine-growers, and drink with them from the full-bellied jug. And there we would always meet with gay companions, for the land is rich and fair, so that in it flourishes untroubled leisure, and wit and humour are its unquestioned coin.

Thus evening after evening we would sit at the festive board. During these weeks masked watchers with rattle and musket patrol the vineyards from morning grey to nightfall and keep the covetous birds in check. It is late when they return festooned with quail, with speckled thrushes and fig-eaters, and soon their booty appears on the table on plates wine-leaf bedecked. Roast chestnuts, too, and fresh walnuts went well with the young wine, and above all the splendid mushrooms, which in those parts they seek out in the woods with dogs – the white truffle, the delicate morel and the red Emperor's sponge.

As long as the wine was sweet and honey-coloured we sat in harmony at the table, conversing peacefully and often with an arm on a neighbour's shoulder. But as soon as it began to work and cast out the baser elements, our vital spirits awoke mightily. Then there were brilliant duels which the weapon of laughter decided, and in which met fencers who shone by their light, untrammelled command of thought – mastery such as comes only from a long life of leisure.

But more highly than those hours which sped in sparkling wit we treasured the quiet homeward path under the deep waters of intoxication through garden and field while the morning dew was already falling on the gay leaves.. Issuing from the Cock Gate of the little town, we saw the shore shine on our right, and on our left, gleaming in the moon-

18

light, rose the Marble Cliffs. Between them stretched the sleeping vine-clad hills in whose slopes the path strayed and was lost.

Round these paths cling memories of clear and wondrous waking which filled us with awe and at the same time rejoiced us. It seemed as if we had emerged on the surface from the depths of life. Like a knocking that wakes us from our sleep, an image would pierce the darkness of our ecstasy – perhaps a buck's horn such as here the peasant mounts on high poles to set up in his plots of ground, perhaps the great horned owl sitting with yellow eyes on the roof-tree of a barn, or a meteor which shot crackling across the firmament. Then it seemed to us as if we had been endowed with a new faculty with which to see the land; we looked out with eyes which have the power to see the gold and crystals in gleaming veins deep under the vitreous earth. Then it would come about that they drew near, grey and shadowy, the aboriginal spirits of the land, who were at home here long before the cloister bells rang out or sod was turned by the plough. Hesitatingly they approached us with rude and wooden features, all sharing in some unfathomable way an expression at once blithe and terrible, and when we saw them our hearts were both startled and deeply touched. At times it seemed as if they would speak with us, but soon they dissolved like smoke.

In silence we traversed the short stretch of road to the Rue-Garden Hermitage. When the light sprang up in the library we would look at one another, and I would perceive in Brother Otho's face the strong, bright glow. It was a mirror from which I learned that the encounter had not been illusory. Without exchanging a word we grasped hands, and I mounted to the herbarium. Nor did we ever further discuss such an experience.

Upstairs I would sit long at the open window in great blitheness of spirit and feel with my inmost heart the stuff of life unwinding from the spindle its golden threads. Then the sun rose over Alta Plana, and radiantly its light spread across the provinces until it reached the Burgundian marches. The wild peaks and glaciers sparkled in white and red, and tremulously the high banks took shape in the green mirror of the Marina.

Now the redstarts began their day on the pointed gable and fed their second brood, whose hungry chirpings were like the whetting of knives. From the reeds that lined the sea rose wisps of duck, and in the garden finch and gold-finch picked the last grapes from the vines. Then I would hear the door of the library open and Brother Otho would step out into the garden to look upon the lilies.

2

But in the spring we caroused like clowns, as is the custom of the land. We drew on motley jesters' smocks of patch-work stuff glinting like plumage, and donned the stiff beak-shaped masks. Then, with the pace of Harlequin and arms flapping like wings, we sprang into the little town where the tree of fools was set up in the old market-place. There in the glow of torches the masked parade took place: the men went as birds, and the women masqueraded in the costly raiment of centuries gone by. They bantered us in high feigned voices that rang like the peal of a musical box, and we replied with shrill bird cries.

Now from the taverns and the coopers' cellars the marches of the feathered guilds began to draw us on – the thin, piercing flutes of the goldfinches, the chirping zithers of the barn owls, the reedy basses of the capercailzies, and the squeaking barrel organs with which the hoopoe frater-nity accompany their scandalous rhymes. Brother Otho and I joined fellowship with the woodpeckers, who beat out their march with cooking spoons on wooden firkins and held clownish council and high court of folly. Here it was well to be guarded in drinking, for we had to draw the wine from the glass with corn-stalks through the nostrils of the beaks. If our heads threatened to turn, a stroll through the gardens and moats of the town wall refreshed us; then, too, we would rove out to the dancing floors, or, pushing back our masks in the arbour of a hostelry, sup from hollow pots in company of a fleeting love a dish of snails in the Burgundian style.

Everywhere in these nights the shrill bird song rang out until the dawn – in the dark lanes and along the great Marina, in the chestnut groves and vineyards, from the lantern-decked gondolas on the dark expanse of the lake, and even among the high cypresses of the burial-grounds. And always, like its echo, one heard the startled, fleeting cry that answered it. The women of this land are fair and possessed of that generosity that old Pulverkopf calls liberal virtue. It is, you know, not the sorrows of this life but its wantonness and its untamed abundance that, when we think of them, bring us near to tears. So this play of voices lies deep in my ear, and above all the suppressed cry with which Lauretta met me on the wall. Although a white-and-gold embroidered hooped dress concealed her limbs and a mother-of-pearl mask her face, I had recognized her at once in the dark alley by the motion of the hips that marked her gait, and slyly I hid behind a tree. Then I startled her with the woodpecker's laugh and pursued her with a fluttering of my wide black sleeves. Up where the Roman stone stands in the wine lands I caught her, exhausted and trembling, pressed her in my arms and bent the fire-red mask over her face. When I felt her resting thus in my clutch, dreaming and spell-bewitched, compassion seized me, and with a smile I pushed the bird mask up on to my brow.

Then she too began to smile, and gently laid her hand on my mouth – so gently that in the stillness I heard only the breath that fluttered through her fingers.

3

But otherwise we lived, day in, day out, in our Rue-Garden Hermitage in great seclusion. The Hermitage stood at the edge of the Marble Cliffs in the middle of one of those rock islands which here and there one sees breaking through the grape land. Its garden had been won from the rock in narrow terraces, and on the sides of its drystone walls wild herbs had settled such as thrive in the fertile vine-growing country. Thus in the early year the blue pearl clusters of the grape hyacinth bloomed, and in autumn the geans rejoiced us with the red Chinese lantern gleam of their fruit. But at all seasons house and garden were ringed with the silvery green rue bushes from which, when the sun was high, a pungent odour rose in swirls.

At midday, when the great heat warmed the grapes to maturity, it was refreshingly cool in the cloister, for not only were its floors laid with mosaics in the southern style, but also many of its rooms extended back into the cliff. Yet at this time I loved to lie stretched on the terrace and listen, half asleep, to the glassy singing of the cicadas. Then the butterflies sailed down into the garden and alit on the saucer blooms of the wild poppies, and on the crags the pearly lizards sunned themselves on the stone. And finally, when the white sand of the snake path flamed in the midday glow, the lance-head vipers drew themselves slowly forward on to it, and soon it was covered with their hieroglyphics like a papyrus roll.

We felt no fear of these beasts which made their homes in swarms among the clefts and crevices of the Rue-Garden Hermitage; on the contrary, by day their iridescence charmed us, and by night the fine resonant piping with which they accompanied their courting. Often we would step over them with clothes slightly caught up, and when we had a visitor who feared them would push them aside with our feet. But invariably we accompanied our guests hand in hand along the snake path; and at such times I noticed that the feeling of freedom and the dancer's sureness that possessed us on this stretch of ground seemed to communicate itself to them.

Many things combined to make the animals so familiar, but had it not been for Lampusa, our old cook, we would have been scarcely aware of their habits. Every evening through all the summer Lampusa put out for them before her rock-hewn kitchen a silver quaich of milk; then she summoned the creatures with a low call. Then over all the garden the golden coils were to be seen glistening in the last rays of the sun – over the dark soil of the lily beds and the silver-grey rue hummocks, and high up in the hazel and elder bushes. Now, forming the blazon of the flaming fire-wheel, they laid themselves round the quaich and received the offering.

Lampusa had early begun to hold little Erio in her arms during the ceremony, and his tiny voice accompanied her call. But what was my amazement one evening to see the child, who could scarcely walk, drag the quaich into the open. There he beat the rim with a pearwood spoon, and the gleaming red snakes came gliding from the clefts of the Marble Cliffs. As if in a waking dream I heard him laugh as he stood amongst them on the trodden clay of the court-yard before the kitchen. Half erect, the creatures played around him and swayed their heavy triangular heads to and fro above his with rapid beat. I stood on the balcony and did not dare to call to my boy, as if he were a sleep-walker wandering on the heights. But then I saw old Lampusa standing with crossed arms before the kitchen door and smiling, and there spread through me the joyous feeling of safety in the burning heart of danger.

From that evening it was Erio who called us with the supper bell. As soon as we heard the ring of the quaich we laid aside our work to watch his offering with delight. Brother Otho hastened from his library and I from the herbarium on the inner gallery. Lampusa, too, forsook her fireside to watch the child with proud and tender look. It was the earnestness with which he disciplined the animals that most amused us. Soon he could call each one by name, and in his gold-embroidered dress of blue velvet would run about within their circle with childish steps. He was careful, too, to see that all received their share of milk, and made room for the late-comers at the quaich. Then with his pear-wood spoon he would beat one or other of the drinkers on the head, or if it did not make way quickly enough seized it by the nape of the neck and dragged it away with might and main. However he might grip them the while, the animals were always gentle and tame with him, even when they were at their most tender at sloughing time. Then the herdsmen will not let their cattle go to pasture near the Marble Cliffs, for a bite that finds its mark fells even the strongest steer with lightning speed.

Above all, Erio loved the biggest and most beautiful of the snakes, which Brother Otho and I called the Griffon, and which – as we learned from the tales of the wine-growers – had had its home in the clefts as long as man could remember. The body of the lance-head viper is metallic red, patterned with scales like burnished brass. But this griffon was cast in pure and faultless golden brilliance, changing at the head to jewel-like green and gaining in lustre. When she was aroused, too, she could swell her neck till it was a shield that sparkled like a golden mirror in the attack. It seemed as if the others did her reverence, for none touched the quaich before the golden one had quenched her thirst. Then we would see little Erio frolicking with her, while, like a kitten, she rubbed her pointed head against his dress.

When it was over Lampusa would bring us our supper – two glasses of common wine and two slices of dark and salty bread.

4

From the terrace one passed through a glass door into the library. In the morning when it was fine this door stood wide open so that Brother Otho, sitting at his great table, seemed to be in a part of the garden. I loved to enter this room where green leafy shadows played on the ceiling while into its stillness penetrated the chirping of the young birds and the nearby humming of the bees.

On its frame by the window stood the wide drawing-board, and on the walls the books towered up in rows to the ceiling. The lowest of them stood on a broad shelf that was cut to the size of the folios – the great Hortus Plantarum Mundi and the hand-illuminated works of which the art is lost. Above them protruded the specimen cases, which could be enlarged by sliding panels, covered with scattered papers mixed with mountings of pressed leaves. Their dark wooden shelves also bore a collection of fossilized plants which we had chiselled out in lime-pits and mines, and scattered through them were numerous crystals laid out for their beauty's sake or for weighing in the hand when talk was deep. Above them rose the small volumes – a not over-extensive collection of botanical works, but one which lacked nothing ever written on lilies. And this section of the library was divided into three classes – into works dealing with form, colour and scent.

The rows of books continued in the small hall and followed the stair that led up into the herbarium. Here stood the church fathers, the thinkers and the classical authors, ancient and modern, and, above all, a collection of dictionaries and encyclopaedias of all kinds. In the evening I would join company with Brother Otho in the little hall where a small fire of vine-cuttings burned in the hearth. If our work prospered during the day we would indulge in that manner of talk in the course of which well-worn paths are trod and dates and authorities acknowledged. We amused ourselves with the curiosities of erudition and with

25

quotations chosen for rarity or a touch of the absurd. Then we were well served by the legion of leather- or parchment-bound slaves.

Usually I went up into the herbarium early in the day and worked on there till after midnight. When we moved into the cloister we had had the floor well laid with wood and had set up long rows of cupboards. In them were heaped in their thousands bundles of mounted flowers. Only a minute proportion of them had been collected by us, and most had been passed on by hands long since turned to dust. At times, when looking for a plant, I would even come across sheets browned by time on which the faded signature was from the pen of the great Master Linnaeus himself. In these night and morning hours I filled in labels and built up the index – first, the great catalogue of the collection and then the Little Flora in which we recorded all our discoveries in the territory of the Marina. On the following day Brother Otho, with the aid of reference books, would check the labels, adding detail or colour. So a work grew, and in its very growing we rejoiced.

When we are happy our senses are contented with however little this world cares to offer. I had long done reverence to the kingdom of plants, and during years of travel had tracked down its wonders. I knew intimately the sensation of that moment when the heart ceases to beat and we divine in a flower's unfolding the mysteries that each grain of seed conceals. Yet the splendour of growth and blossoming was never nearer to me than when I trod this room with its wafted scent of long-withered greenery.

Before I laid myself to rest I would pace up and down a while in its narrow centre aisle. Often at these midnight hours I seemed to see the plants more brilliant and more splendid than ever before. From afar I caught the fragrance of the white-starred thorny valleys where I had drunk in the bitter springtide of Arabia Deserta, or the scent of vanilla which refreshes the wanderer in the shadeless furnace of the candelabra woods. Then there opened up like the pages of some old book memories of hours spent amidst savage profusion – of hot marshes where the Victoria Regia blooms, of tidal groves seen sweltering at noon on their pale stilts far from the palm-lined coast. Yet I felt none of that fear which seizes us when we face the prodigality of nature's growth and see in it the alluring thousand-armed image of a god. I felt that through our studies the power increased to hold at bay the forces of life like a steed on the curb.

Often the dawn was showing grey before I stretched myself on the narrow camp bed that was set up in the herbarium.

5

Lampusa's kitchen stretched far back into the Marble Cliff. In times gone by such caves provided shelter and lodging for the herdsmen, and later were included within the precincts of the farmsteads. Early in the morning when she was cooking Erio's gruel one would see the old woman standing by the fire. Still deeper vaults led off from the kitchen; in them there was the scent of milk, of fruit and oozing wine. It was seldom that I entered this part of the Hermitage, for the presence of Lampusa awoke in me a feeling of constraint that I preferred to avoid. But Erio knew every nook and corner.

Brother Otho, too, I would often see standing with the old woman by the fire. To him I owed the happiness that had been my lot with Erio, the love-child of Silvia, Lampusa's daughter. In those days we were in service with the Purple Horse in the abortive campaign against the free peoples of Alta Plana. Often when we rode up to the passes we would see Lampusa standing before her hut with at her side the slender figure of Silvia in her red head-cloth and red skirt. Brother Otho was with me when I gathered from the dust the carnation which Silvia had taken from her hair and thrown in our path. As we rode on he warned me – mockingly, but with an undertone of anxiety – against witches, old and young. But I was more nettled by the laughter of Lampusa, who scanned me with a glance in which I saw the shamelessness of a bawd. And yet it was not long before I frequented her hut.

When we returned to the Marina on our discharge and moved into the Hermitage we learned of the child's birth, learned, too, that Silvia had abandoned it and travelled off with strangers. The news disturbed me all the more since it affected me at the beginning of a period when, after the sufferings of the campaign, I wished to dedicate my days to quiet studies.

And so I gave Brother Otho full powers to seek out Lampusa, consult with her, and grant her what seemed fit to him. What was my astonishment to learn that he had taken the child and herself into our household; and yet this step soon proved to be a blessing for us all. And since one may recognize the justice of an action from the fact that through it the past finds its fulfilment, so now my love for Silvia appeared to me in a new light. I recognized that I had been prejudiced against both her and her mother, and, finding her light, had dealt with her all too lightly, taking for mere glass a jewel that sparkled on the open road. Yet everything of price falls to us by chance; the best is unpaid for.

Admittedly, to achieve this equilibrium that open-mindedness was necessary which was Brother Otho's by nature. It was a basic principle with him to treat each single person with whom we came into contact as a rare find discovered on one's travels. Then, too, his favourite name for men was 'the optimates', to signify that everyone must be numbered among the true-born nobility of this world, and that from any one of them we may receive supreme gifts. To him they were vessels stored with wonders, and to figures of such nobility he accorded the rights of princes. And in truth I saw how each one who approached him unfolded like a plant awaking from its winter sleep; it was not that they became better, but that they became more themselves.

28

As soon as she had settled in, Lampusa took charge of the housekeeping. The work was no labour to her, and in the garden too she had green fingers. Whereas Brother Otho and I planted strictly according to rules, she casually laid the seed under a dusting of earth and let the weeds riot at will. And yet without exertion she harvested three times our winnings in seed and fruit. Often I would see her look with a mocking smile at the oval porcelain boards in our beds which bore the name and species in Brother Otho's fine sign-painter's hand. Then, like an old boar, she would bare the last great incisor that remained to her.

Although, like Erio, I called her Grandmother, she spoke to me almost entirely of household matters, often in the foolish vein that housekeepers adopt. Silvia's name was never mentioned. Yet I was ill at ease when, the evening after the night on the wall, Lauretta came to fetch me away. The old woman, on the other hand, showed marked high spirits, and hastened to bring out wine, titbits and sweetmeats for the visitor.

In Erio I discovered the natural pleasure of a parent and the spiritual one of an adoptive father. We loved his quiet, noticing nature. Since all children have the habit of imitating the activities they see in their small world, he early became interested in plants. Often we would see him sit for hours on the terrace watching a lily on the point of unfolding, and when the bloom had opened he would hasten into the library to rejoice Brother Otho with the news. So, too, he loved to stand in the early morning beside the marble basin in which we reared water-roses from Zipangu whose blooms burst their sheath with a scarcely audible noise at the first touch of the sun. In the herbarium, too, I had provided a little chair for him, on which he often sat and watched me at my work. When I felt him sitting quietly at my side I seemed to be refreshed, as if things had acquired a new light from the deep bright flame that burned in his little body. And it seemed to me as if animals were drawn to him; for instance, I noticed every time I met him in the garden how the ladybirds flew round him, running over his hands and playing around his hair. Strange, too, was the fact that the vipers, when called by Lampusa, surrounded the quaich in mixed and glowing braids, whereas with Erio they formed a rayed wheel. This Brother Otho was the first to notice.

So it came about that our life diverged from the plans that we had spun. But we noticed that this divergence caused the work to prosper.

6

We had arrived with the plan of studying plant life intensively, and had therefore begun in accordance with old and well-tried methodology with their breathing and nourishment. Like all things of this earth, plants too attempt to speak to us, but one requires sharp senses to understand their speech. Although in their seeding, blooming and decay there lies hid the illusion which nothing created may escape, yet one may easily discern the unchanging quality that lies locked within the outward show of things. The art of rendering one's sight thus keen Brother Otho called 'sucking time dry'; but he was of the mind that this side of death the cup cannot be drained.

After we had settled down we discovered that our thesis had extended in scope almost against our will. Perhaps it was the strong air of the Rue-Garden Hermitage that gave our thought a new twist, just as a flame burns bolder and brighter in a pure gas. So even after the first few weeks it seemed to me as if external things were being transformed; and the transformation first manifested itself to me as an inability to express myself in words.

One morning as I looked out on to the Marina from the terrace, her waters appeared to me deeper and more translucent, as if I were seeing them for the first time with unclouded vision. At the same moment I felt, almost with anguish, words and phenomena springing apart like the cord from an over-taut bow. I had seen a fragment of the iridescent veil of this world, and from that hour my tongue failed me.

At the same time, however, a new awareness possessed me. Like a child groping with its hands when the light of its eyes is first directed out upon the world, I cast around for words and images to catch the new splendour which dazzled me. I had never before divined that speech itself could be such a torment, and yet I did not regret the old and care-free life. If we dream of flying, a clumsy spring brings us more joy than the security of well-trod paths. It is thus, too, that I explain the sensation of giddiness which often assailed me during my attempts.

When we seek out unknown ways it is easy to lose sense of balance. So I was fortunate in Brother Otho's company as he moved forward by my side with guarded step. Often when I had fathomed the mystery of a word I would hasten down to him, pen in hand, and often he mounted to the herbarium on the same errand. We took pleasure, too, in forming images, which we called 'models', formed by writing on a piece of paper four or five phrases in light metre. Through them we aimed to fix a fragment of this world's mosaic like a stone mounted in metal. For these models we had begun with plants, and continually returned to them. Thus we described objects and their metamorphoses, from the grain of sand to the cliff of marble, and from the fleeting second to the changing year. In the evening we would collect our scraps, and when we had read them would burn them on the hearth.

Soon we felt our energies increasing, and a new sureness possessed us. The word is both king and magician. Our high example we found in Linnaeus, who went out into the unruly world of plants and animals with the word as his sceptre of state. And more wonderful than any sword-won empire, his power extends over the flowering fields and nameless insect hosts.

Thus we, too, were driven on by the presentiment that order reigns among the elements; for man feels impelled to imitate creation with his feeble faculties, as a bird is driven to build its nest. And our labours were abundantly rewarded with the revelation that rule and measure are imbedded in the hazards and disorders of this earth. As we climb, we draw nearer to that secret whose final mysteries are hidden in the dust. So with every upward step the chance pattern of the horizon is lost among the mountains, but when we have climbed sufficiently it encircles us on every hand, whatever our point of vantage, with the pure ring that unites us to eternity.

It is true that our achievements in this field remained prentice work and childish learning; yet we felt our joy increase, as it must in anyone whose goal is set beyond the common mark. The landscape of the Marina lost its dazzling quality, but gained in clarity and definition. The days flowed by with stronger, swifter current, like water that has found its course. Occasionally when the west wind blew we seemed to savour in anticipation the pleasures of unshadowed joy.

Above all, we lost something of that fear that beset us and troubled our minds like a marsh mist. Thus it came about that our work was not abandoned when the Chief Ranger seized power in our territory and terror spread throughout the land.

7

We had long known the Chief Ranger as a grand master of Mauretania. We had often seen him at junketings, and diced and wined with him through many a night. He was one of those figures whom the Mauretanians respect as great lords and yet find somewhat ridiculous – rather as an old colonel of the mounted yeomanry is received in the regiment on his occasional visits from his estates. He left an imprint on one's memory, if only because his green coat with its gold-embroidered ilex leaves drew all eyes to him.

His wealth was rumoured to be boundless, and at the banquets which he gave in his town house profusion reigned. There, in the old style, drinking was hard and stakes were high, so that the oak boards of the great gaming table groaned under its load of gold. Famous, too, were the oriental suppers in his little villas, to which were invited the favoured few. Thus I had frequent opportunities to see him close at hand, and felt the breath of primitive power that surrounded him like a breeze from his forests. At this period I was scarcely disturbed by the inflexibility of his nature, for all Mauretanians acquire with time something of the nature of an automaton. This characteristic is particularly marked in their glance, and so the eyes of the Chief Ranger, too – especially when he laughed – gleamed with terrifying mirth. Like those of hardened drinkers, they were touched with a red flame, but expressed both cunning and unshakeable power – yes, at times even majesty. Then we took pleasure in his company and lived in arrogance at the table of the great ones of the world.

Later I was to hear Brother Otho say of our Mauretanian period that mistakes become errors only when persisted in. It was a saying that gained in truth for me when I thought back to our position when this Order attracted us. There are periods of decline when the pattern fades to which our inmost life must conform. When we enter upon them we sway and lose our balance. From hollow joy we sink to leaden sorrow, and past and future acquire a new charm from our sense of loss. So we wander aimlessly in the irretrievable past or in distant Utopias; but the fleeting moment we cannot grasp.

As soon as we had become aware of this failure we strove to free ourselves. We felt a longing for actuality, for reality, and would have plunged into ice or fire or ether only to rid ourselves of weariness. As always when despair and maturity combine, we turned to power – for is that not the eternal pendulum that drives on the hand of time by day or night? So we began to dream of power and domination, and of the forms that in bold array advance to combat in the deadly struggle for existence, whether the outcome be disaster or triumphant victory. We studied them with the pleasure one finds in watching corrosions form as acid bites into dark mirrors of polished metal. Such being our inclination, it was inevitable that the Mauretanians should seek us out. Our sponsor was the Condottiere who had put down the rising in the Iberian provinces.

Anyone acquainted with the history of the secret Orders knows that their ramifications are difficult to assess. Similarly it is common knowledge with what fertility they form branches and colonies, so that attempts to trace them down end in a maze. For the Mauretanians too this held good. To the newcomer it was particularly strange to see in their meeting-places members of deadly hostile groups in friendly conversation. Among the aims of the Mauretanians was artistry in the dealings of this world. They demanded that power should be exercised dispassionately as by a god, and correspondingly its schools produced a race of spirits who were bright, untrammelled, but always terrible. Similarly, whether their duties lay in insurrection or in order, wherever they won the day they won it as Mauretanians, and the proud 'Semper victrix' of this Order applied not only to its members, but to its head and fount of doctrine. Immovable among the wild currents of the times he stood, and in his residences and palaces one was on firm ground.

It was not because we enjoyed peace, however, that we willingly spent our time with them. When man loses his props fear begins to sway him, and he is driven along blindly in its whirlwinds. But with the Mauretanians absolute stillness reigned, as in the heart of a cyclone. They say that if one falls headlong into an abyss one sees things in the minutest detail as though through a crystal-clear lens. This – without the fear – was the vision that one acquired in the air of Mauretania, in an atmosphere which was poisoned through and through. At the very moment when terror reigned, coolness of thought and spiritual detachment increased. In the face of catastrophe good-humour was everywhere, and they would jest at it like the keeper of a gaming-table at the losses of his clients.

Then I saw clearly that the panic whose shadows always lie over our great towns has its counterpart in the cool audacity of the few who circle like birds of prey over inarticulate suffering. Once when we were drinking with the Condottiere he looked into his wine-dewed glass as if it were a mirror that held the images of times long past; then he said pensively: 'No glass of noble wine was more precious than the one they handed to us beside our machines the night we burned Saguntum to the ground.' Then we thought: It is better to fall with him than live with those who grovel in the dust from fear.

But this is away from my story. Among the Mauretanians one could learn the sports that still delight such spirits as have broken all bonds and are sated even with mockery. For them the world was no more than a map charted for connoisseurs with the aid of metal discs and shining instruments, to handle which is a pleasure in itself. Therefore it seemed strange to find in this clear, unshadowed and most abstract of realms figures like the Chief Ranger. Yet wherever free spirits establish their sway these primeval powers will always join their company like a snake creeping to the open fire. They are the old connoisseurs of power who see a new day dawning in which to re-establish the tyranny that has lived in their hearts since the beginning of time. Thus there develop in the great Orders secret and subterranean channels in which the historian is lost. Subtle conflicts break out and smoulder in the innermost seats of power, conflicts between symbols and theories, conflicts between idols and spirits.

In the course of such conflicts it has been the lot of many to trace the knavery of this world to its source. Such, too, had been my experience when I penetrated into the Chief Ranger's hunting-grounds in search of long-lost Fortunio. From that time on I learned the limits which no audacity may overstep, and shunned the dark fringe of the forest which their master loved to call his 'Teutoburger Wald';

for he was a master of feigning frankness that was full of snares for the unwary.

8

During my search for Fortunio I had penetrated the northern edge of these woods, whereas our Hermitage lay near their southern extremity which marches with Burgundy. On our return we found only a shadow of the old way of life by the Marina. Up till then it had held sway almost unaltered since the time of Charlemagne, for whatever overlords might come or go, the wine-growers remained sober and law-abiding. Then, too, the richness and luxury of the soil tempered every overlordship to mildness, however harsh it might at first have been. Such is the effect of beauty on power.

But the war on the borders of Alta Plana, waged as if against the infidel, had had a more profound effect, ravaging like a frost that splits a tree to the core, but whose effect is first apparent only years later. That was how life developed by the Marina. It was the old life, and yet something had changed in it. Sometimes when we stood on the terrace and looked out on to the encircling gardens we seemed to catch a breath of hidden listlessness and anarchy. It was then that the beauty of the land touched our hearts with pain. Thus the colours of life stand out in final splendour before the sun sinks.

At first we heard little of the Chief Ranger; but it was noteworthy how as lassitude set in and reality dissolved he drew ever nearer. At first one heard only rumours like the first obscure heralds of a pest raging in distant harbours. Then reports spread from mouth to mouth of infringements of the law and of acts of violence in the neighbourhood, and finally such incidents occurred publicly and with no attempt at concealment. A cloud of fear preceded the Chief Ranger like the mountain mist that presages the storm. Fear enveloped him, and I am convinced that therein far more than in his own person, lay his power. Only when things had begun to totter from their inherent weakness could he exercise his might; but when that moment came his forests were well placed for assault against the land.

If one climbed to the summit of the Marble Cliffs one could look down on to the entire expanse of territory over which he aimed to dominate. To reach the peak we used to clamber up the narrow staircase hollowed from the rock beside Lampusa's kitchen. Its rain-washed steps led out on to a projecting ledge from which to view the country round as far as the eye could see. Here we lingered many an hour in the sun while the cliffs sparkled with colour, for where the trickling water ate at the dazzling white stone it had taken on red and yellow lights. Dark ivy hung in heavy curtains, and in the damp crevices there sparkled the silver leaves of lunaria.

During the ascent our feet would catch on the bramble creepers and startle the lizards, which fled with a flash of green among the crags. Up where the overhang was deep in turf, sown with blue-starred gentians, were crystal-edged cavities in whose recesses owls blinked dreamily. There, too, the swift rust-brown falcons nested; we passed so close to their broods that we saw the nostrils in their beaks and the fine skin that covered them like a film of blue wax.

Up here on the summit the air was fresher than below in the hollow, where the vines shimmered in the heat. Occasionally the heat forced up a gust of air that whistled in the rock chimneys as if they were organ pipes, and brought with it traces of rose, almond and balm. From our perch on the cliffs we saw the roof of the cloister far below us. To the south beyond the Marina, Alta Plana towered behind its ring of glaciers. Often its peaks were shrouded by mist rising from the water, at other times the air was so clear that we could distinguish the conifers which push far up into the scree. On such days we felt the storm brewing and put out our house fires over night.

Often our glance would rest on the islands of the Marina,

which we jokingly called the Hesperides, and whose shores were dark with cypresses. Even in the hardest winters frost or snow are unknown there; figs and oranges ripen in the open and roses bloom through the year. When almond and apricot are in bloom the people of the Marina love to be rowed across the water; then the isles are like gay petals on the blue surface of the stream. In the autumn, again, they sail across to eat St Peter's fish, which rise to the surface from the depths when the moon is full, and strain the nets with their shoals. The fishers lay their nets in silence, for they hold that even a whisper will frighten off the fish, and that an oath will ruin the catch. These fish-eating excursions were always merry ones; one went provisioned with bread and wine, for the vine does not bear well on the islands. There there are no cool autumn nights when the dew falls on the grapes and their fiery spirit quickens with a presentiment of decay.

To understand what is meant by living one had to look down to the Marina on one of these gay holidays. Early in the morning the whole gamut of noises rose up to us, fine and distinct, like objects seen through a reversed spy-glass. We heard the bells of the towns and the petards saluting the flag-dressed ships in the harbours, or it would be the hymns of pious processions going on pilgrimage to miraculous images, or the music of the flutes in a bridal train. We heard the chatter of the daws around the weathercocks, the crowing of cocks, the call of cuckoos, the horns of hunters riding out from the town gate to hawk the heron. All mounted up to us in harmonies so quaint that the whole world seemed to be merely a brilliant patchwork; the effect was as heady as wine drunk fasting.

Far below lay the Marina, edged with little towns with walls and watch towers dating from Roman times; high above them rose age-grey cathedrals and Merovingian castles. Between came rich villages with clouds of pigeons circling round their roofs, and mills green with moss towards which in the autumn one saw the asses being driven with their loads of corn. Then castles again nestling on high crags, and monasteries where the light was mirrored in the carp ponds round their walls.

When from our lofty perch we looked down on the structures man had raised for his protection and his pleasure, to store his food or to contain his gods, the centuries fused before our eyes into a single span. And, as if the graves had opened, the dead rose up invisibly. They are always near to us when we look upon a land we love, in which an ancient culture has its roots; and just as their heritage lives on in stone and tillage, their ancient spirit rules over meadow and field.

At our backs towards the north ran the marches of the Campagna, separated from the Marina by the wall of marble cliffs. In spring its fringe of meadows stretched like a flowered carpet in which the herds browsed and seemed to swim in coloured foam. At midday they rested in the cool and muddy shade of the alders and aspens, which formed leafy islands on the wide plain, from which often there rose the smoke of herdsmen's fires. Scattered far apart one could see the big farms with their stalls and barns, and the high poles of the wells which feed the drinking-troughs.

Here in summer it was hot and misty, and in autumn, when the snakes couple, the whole stretch was like a deserted steppe – lonely and parched. At its farther border the ground changed to marshland with thick growth in which there was no sign of human habitation. Only duck-hunters' huts of coarse reeds rose here and there beside the dark moorland water; in the alders were concealed perches built like crows' nests. This was already land where the writ of the Chief Ranger ran, and soon the ground began to rise in which the forest had its roots. From its fringes there projected into the pasturage long sickle-shaped thickets which in the people's speech were called 'horns'.

Such was the kingdom which offered itself to the view, and by which the Marble Cliffs were encircled. From their heights we saw life developing on ancient ground like the vines, orderly and well trained, and bearing fruit. And we saw its frontiers too: the mountains where lofty freedom but not plenty found its home among the barbarian peoples, and towards the north the swamps and the dark recesses where bloody tyranny lurked.

Often, aloft on the crags, we reflected how much labour it costs before the grain is harvested and the bread baked, and how much too before the spirit can stretch its wings in safety.

9

In prosperous times little attention was paid to the feuds which had always been a feature of life in the Campagna; rightly so, for they ever recur where there are herds and pasture lands. Every spring there were quarrels over the still unbranded cattle, and, whenever droughts began, fights at the water-holes. The great steers, too, with ringed nostrils, which troubled the dreams of the women by the Marina, would break into strange herds and chase them to the Marble Cliffs, at the foot of which one saw their bleaching horns and bones.

Above all, the race of herdsmen was wild and unruly. From the beginning of time their calling had been handed down from father to son, and when they sat round their fires in ragged dress with rude weapons of stone or wood one saw how different they were from the race which cultivates the vineyard slopes. Their way of life belonged to the times when house and plough and loom were still unknown, and nomads' shelters were constructed as the wanderings of the herds required. To this their customs corresponded – their rough sense of justice and equality based on talion law. So every killing fanned long-burning fires of revenge, and there were tribal and family feuds of which the origins were unknown, and which nevertheless yearly extorted their tribute of blood. 'Campagna cases' was the name given by the lawyers of the Marina to uncivilised and tangled suits brought before them; and they did not summon the herdsmen to the forum, but sent out commissioners into their territory. In other districts justice was dispensed by the tenants of the magnates and lords of the manor living on their great cattle farms. In addition there were free herdsmen, rich in stock, like the Bataks and the Belovars.

Contact with this rough race revealed their good qualities; among these was conspicuous the hospitality which surrounded everyone who sat by their fires. So it came about that one might see in their circles the faces of town-dwellers, for the Campagna offered immediate shelter to all who had to quit the Marina under a cloud. Here one met debtors threatened with arrest and scholars who had planted too shrewd a blow at a drinking party, all in company with renegade monks and a crew of vagabonds. Young people, too, who longed for freedom and pairs of lovers willingly betook themselves to the Campagna.

So at all seasons a web of secrecy was spun which extended beyond the boundaries of law and order. The nearness of the Campagna, in which justice took less constitutional forms, was an advantage to many whose affairs had taken an unfavourable turn. Most returned when time and good friends had worked in their favour, and others disappeared into the woods never to be seen again. But after Alta Plana what had once been the normal course of affairs took an unhealthy turn. Thus in exhausted bodies corruption will set in by way of wounds which a sound man would scarcely notice.

The first symptoms, therefore, were not recognized. When rumours of disturbances poured in from the Campagna it seemed that the old blood feuds had become more bitter, but soon it was noticeable that they were obscured by new and unusual traits. The core of rough honour which had tempered violence was destroyed, and mere crime remained. One had the impression, too, that spies and agents from the forests had penetrated the clans to use them for unknown purposes. In this way the old forms lost their sense.

For example, there had never been any doubt when a corpse was found at a cross-roads, its tongue split by a dagger, that here a traitor had fallen to the vengeance of his trackers. After the war, too, one might stumble on such corpses, but now it was common knowledge that these were the victims of criminal murder.

Similarly the tribes had always levied blackmail, but the landowners had paid it gladly, regarding it as a sort of premium on the well-being of their grazing herds. But now the tribute grew unbearably, and when the farmer saw the demand letter flutter white on a post he had to pay or flee the country. Many had, indeed, thought of resistance, but in such cases plunderings had occurred which were apparently conducted according to a considered plan.

Then a rabble led by men of the forests would appear at night before the farmsteads, and were entrance denied, broke down the gates. These bands were also known as 'glow-worms', for they attacked the doors with beams hung with small lights. Others derived the name from their habit, once they had won ingress, of torturing the people with fire to learn where the silver was hidden. At all events, there were tales which laid at their door the lowest and basest acts of which man is capable. To these belonged their method of instilling fear by packing the corpses of murdered men in chests or barrels; such gruesome consignments were then delivered to the relatives by transports coming from the Campagna.

Far more menacing still was the fact that all these crimes, which set the land in an uproar and cried for justice, went almost entirely unavenged. It even came to such a pass that nobody dared any longer speak of them openly, and it became clear how weak the law was in comparison to anarchy. It is true that shortly after the pillaging began the commissioners had been sent out, accompanied by pickets, but they had found the Campagna already in open revolt, so that there could be no question of negotiation. Now in order to take strong measures the estates had to be convoked according to the constitution, for in countries which, like the Marina, have a long legal tradition the course of justice is not willingly abandoned.

Thereupon it became apparent that the men of the Campagna already had their representatives in the Marina, for returning citizens had either retained business connections with the herdsman or joined the clans by taking the blood oath. This group, too, followed the change for evil, particularly wherever order was already undermined.

So it came about that shady advocates sprang up who defended the cause of injustice before the Bar, and in the little harbour taverns the clansmen openly made their lairs. At their tables sights were to be seen like those out at the camp fires; there old herdsmen with untanned skins thrown round their legs squatted beside officers who since Alta Plana had idled on half-pay. There whoever among the people from either side of the Marble Cliffs were malcontent or greedy for change caroused and thronged the doors as if in the dark interiors lay their headquarters.

It could not but add to the confusion that even sons of notables and youths who believed that the hour of a new freedom had dawned took part in this traffic. So, too, there were men of letters who began to imitate the herdsmen's songs, which up to now only the nurses from the Campagna had been known to croon over the cradles. But now the poets might be seen strolling in the Corso with rough cudgels in their hands, and wearing shaggy skins instead of woollen or linen raiment. In such circles it was the custom to scorn the tillage of vine or corn and to see in the wild country of the herdsmen the stronghold of the true, time-honoured way of life. They are well known, the hare-brained and somewhat murky ideas which bewitch the enthusiast, and one might have laughed at them had it not come to open sacrilege which passed the understanding of all who still had kept their reason.

10

In the Campagna where the meadow paths crossed the grazing boundaries one often saw standing the little herdsmen's gods. These guardians of the marches were rudely cut from stone or oak and even from a distance one guessed their presence from the rancid smell they spread abroad. For the offerings brought to them consisted of libations of melted butter and fat from the entrails pushed aside by the sacrificial knife. That was why one always saw round the images black scars of fires in the green pastureland. After their offering, the herdsmen kept a charred stick from the fires with which to mark on the night of the solstice the body of every creature that should bear young, whether heifer or wife.

If on such a spot we met the young girls returning from the milking they would draw their head-cloths over their faces, and Brother Otho, who knew and loved the gods of the garden, never passed by without doing mock homage to the images. He held that they were of great antiquity, and called them Jupiter's childhood companions.

Then, too, there was not far from the Flayer's Wood a copse of weeping willows, in which stood the figure of a steer with red nostrils, red tongue and red sexual organ. It was a spot of ill-fame, one to which there clung rumours of grisly rites.

But who could have believed that the butter- and fat-fed gods who filled the udders of the cows would now begin to be worshipped on the Marina? Yet so it came about in houses where offerings and their ritual had long been held in mockery. Men who had deemed themselves strong-minded enough to cut the links with the faith of their fathers fell under the yoke and spell of barbarian idols. The sight they offered in their blindness was more loathsome than drunkenness at noon. Thinking to fly and boasting of their powers, they grovelled in the dust.

It was a bad sign, too, that the spirit of disorder laid hold upon the last rites of the dead. At all times the guild of poets had been held in high honour on the Marina. They passed for givers of largesse, and the gift of rhyming was regarded as the source of plenty. That the vine bloomed and bore fruit, that man and beast throve, that the evil winds were calmed and joyous concord lived in the hearts of men – all were ascribed to the melody that lives in song and hymn. Of this the lowliest peasant was convinced, just as he was that harmony has powers to heal.

There lived no one so poor that the first and best fruits of his garden did not go to the cabin of the thinker and the hermitage of the poet. Thus whoever felt called upon to serve the world in things spiritual could live at leisure – in poverty, perhaps, but not in need. In the to-and-fro of life the tillers of soil and the shapers of words found their precept in the old saying: The best gifts of the gods are unpaid for.

It is a sign of good times that in them the power of the spirit is outwardly and visibly manifest. So it was here: no festival in the changing year, in the litany or in the life of man was possible without poetry. But particularly at funeral services, after the corpse had been blessed, it fell to the poet to pass judgement on the dead. It was his task to cast a godlike glance over the departed life and praise it in verse, like the diver prising the pearl from its shell.

From the beginnings of time there had been two measures in which to honour the dead; of these the more usual was the elegeion. The elegeion was held a fit offering to a life led justly in sorrow and in joy such as is the lot of common man. In tone it was a lament, yet it gave full expression to that confidence which comforts the sorrowing heart.

On the other hand there was the eburnum, which in olden days was reserved for the slayers of monsters that dwelt in the swamps and crags. The classical eburnum had to be delivered with high style and noble joy; its peroration was the Admiratio, during which a black eagle soared up from a broken cage. As the times grew milder the eburnum was granted also to those who were known as builders of the state, or 'optimates'. The people had always known in their hearts who belonged to this number, although as life became more refined the images of their forefathers altered too.

But now for the first time the day was seen when conflicts broke out over the speeches delivered by the judges of the dead. For with the leagues, the blood feuds of the Campagna found their way into the towns. Like a pest which finds virgin soil, hate grew apace. There were clashes by night with ignoble weapons for no other reason than that a hundred years before Wenzel had been struck down by Jegor. But reason is nothing when passion blinds us. So soon no night passed by but that the watch came upon dead in the streets and in the houses, and many were found with wounds unworthy of the sword – yes, even showing how blind hate had mangled the fallen foe.

In these fights, which led to man-hunts, ambushes and arson, the parties lost all control. Soon one had the impression that they hardly regarded one another any longer as human beings, and their speech was shot through with words fit to be used only of vermin that must be harried and stamped out with fire and sword. Only in their opponents could they recognize murder; yet they themselves vaunted of things which in the others they despised. While one held the other's dead scarcely worthy of hasty burial in the dead of night, their own were to be shrouded in purple, the eburnum was to sound out and the eagle soar, bearing to the gods a living image of the hero and prophet.

It is true that none of the great singers was prepared to take part in such sacrilege even if offered untold wealth in gold. Then were brought forward the harpists who accompany the dance at kermess festivals, and the blind zither players, who before the tricliniums of the houses of joy delight the drunken guests with songs of Venus' Scallopshell or Hercules the Glutton. Thus warrior and bard were worthy of each other.

But metre, as is known, is incorruptible. The fires of destruction cannot reach its invisible pillars and portals. So

46

they were themselves duped who thought that offerings of the worth of an eburnum could be bought and sold. We attended only the first of these funeral rites, and saw happen what we had awaited. The hireling who was to tread the lofty fragile flaming arch of the poem began at once to stammer and lost his thread. Then his speech gained in fluency and turned to the base iambs of hate and vengeance which spat their venom in the dust. During the scene we saw the crowd in the red festal raiment which is worn for the eburnum, and the magistrates and clergy too in robes of state. Formerly when the eagle soared silence reigned; this time there was an outburst of wild rejoicing.

At the sound sorrow gripped us, and many another too, for we felt that the wholesome spirit of our ancestors had abandoned the Marina.

11

There were many other signs, too, which spelt downfall. They were like a rash which appears, dies down and breaks out again. From time to time life was shot through with care-free days on which everything seemed to be as before.

Herein, above all, lay a masterly trait of the Chief Ranger. He administered fear in small doses which he gradually increased, and which aimed at crippling resistance. The role he played in the disorders which were so finely spun in the heart of his woods was that of a power for order; for while his agents of lower rank, who had established themselves in the clans, fostered anarchy, the initiated penetrated into the civic offices and the magistracy, and there won the reputation of men of deeds who would bring the mob to its senses. Thus the Chief Ranger was like an evil doctor who first encourages the disease so that he may practise on the sufferer the surgery he has in mind.

It is true that among the magistrates there were some clear-headed enough to see through the game, but they had not the power to hinder it. On the Marina it had long been the custom to maintain mercenary troops, and so long as things were orderly they were good servants. But now that the disturbances were stretching up to its banks everyone tried to win over the soldiery, and Biedenhorn, their commander, grew overnight to great importance. It could suit him but little to check a turn in affairs which was so favourable to himself; on the contrary, he began to make difficulties and held back the troops as if they were capital that bore good interest. He had taken up position with them in an old fort, the Barbican, and there he lived like a mouse in cheese. Thus in the vault of one of the great towers he had set up a drinking-hall where he sat at his ease over his cups behind the fortress walls. In the bright glass of the window his coat of arms could be seen – two wassail horns with the motto:

> Come troll
> The bowl!

In this retreat he took up his abode, full of that jovial cunning of the North which it is so easy to underestimate, and there gave audience to the plaintiffs with an air of well-feigned concern. In his cups he was zealous for justice and order – but he was never seen to come to deeds. Besides, he treated not only with the clans, but with the captains of the Chief Ranger too, plying them with meat and drink at the expense of the Marina. With these forest captains he played the communities an evil trick. Making out that he was in need of aid, he entrusted to them and their woodland crew the surveillance of the country districts. Thereby terror had complete sway under the mask of order.

At first the forces under the captains were modest and employed singly as gendarmes. This was true in particular of the Huntsmen whom we often saw patrolling round the Rue-Garden Hermitage, and who, alas! would also sup in Lampusa's kitchen. These were the men of the brushwood of whom one reads in books, small, with eyes that blinked against the light, and with dark beards hanging from their

48

gaunt cheeks; their speech was an argot that drew upon the lowest in all languages and was a compound of blood and scum.

We found that they were equipped with paltry weapons – with nooses, snares and curved daggers which they called 'blood-letters'. Then, too, they were generally hung about with the pelts of vermin. For instance, they gave chase to the great lizards on our stairway in the Marble Cliffs, catching them with the old trick of a fine snare moistened with spittle. The beautiful creatures had often delighted our eyes with their golden-green and dazzling white-starred skin, particularly when we caught sight of them in the bramble bushes which made a red curtain on the cliffs. The foreign courtesans whom the Ranger kept in his courts set great store by the skins, and his fops and dandies had fashioned from them girdles and dainty wallets. So the green wonders were mercilessly pursued and treated with evil cruelty. These torturers did not even trouble to kill them, but robbed the skin from the still living animals and let them fall headlong from the cliffs like white ghosts and end their days in torment at their foot. In base hearts there lies deep-seated a burning hatred of beauty.

Such carrion-catching ploys were a mere pretext for spying about farmstead and house to see whether in them some spark of freedom was yet alive. Then the cases of banditry which were familiar from the Campagna recurred and the inhabitants were led away under cover of darkness and mist. Thence no one returned; and what we heard rumoured among the people of their fate reminded us of the carcasses of the lizards lying stripped below the cliffs, and filled our hearts with sadness.

Then the Foresters too made their appearance, and were often to be seen at work on the vineyard slopes and hills. They seemed to be surveying the land anew, for they had holes dug in the ground and set up rods with runic signs and animal totems. The way they moved about in field and meadow was even more alarming than the Huntsmen's was, for they traversed old tilth as if it were moorland, heeding neither bridle path nor boundary. Nor did they salute the holy images. Thus one saw them cross and recross the rich farmland as if it were desert, uninhabited and barren.

From such signs one could guess what was to be awaited from the Ranger lurking in his forests. He who hated the plough, the corn, the vine and the animals tamed by man, who looked with distaste on spacious dwellings and a free and open life, set little store by lordship over such plenty. Only then did his heart stir when moss and ivy grew green on the ruins of the towns, and under the broken tracery of vaulted cathedrals the bats fluttered in the moon. His forest would spread until the great trees bathed their roots in the Marina, and above their crowns the silver heron would meet the black stork on the wing from the oak thickets to the swamps. In the dark soil of the vineyard slopes the tusked boar would root, and on the cloister ponds the beaver circle, while in the dusk the game came down to water along the hidden paths. And on the edges of the forest where the trees could find no root in the swamps the snipe would flicker in the early year, and in the fall the thrushes come seeking the red berries.

12

Then, too, the Chief Ranger loved neither farmsteads nor poets' hermitages, nor any spot where men spend their days in quiet thought. The best among the dwellers on his domains were yet another race of uncouth varlets whose greatest joy in life was to track the game and bring it to bay. Father and son, they were his men. These were his masters of woodcraft, while the huntsmen of lower rank whom we saw on the Marina hailed from strange villages which the master maintained in the forest depths.

Fortunio, who knew the Ranger's dominions best, had described them to me as warrens of hovels grey with age, their walls built from mud and wattle, and the pointed roofs covered with yellowing moss. There, free as the birds, a brood of darkness had their cavern homes. When this folk was on its wanderings a sect always remained behind in their nests and grottos, like the last grounds one leaves in a jar of spice to preserve its odour.

Into these forest lands had taken flight all who in peace or war had escaped extinction – Huns, Tartars, gipsies, Albigensians and heretical sects of all sorts. With them had joined company fugitives from the provost-marshal and the hangman, scattered remnants of the great robber bands from Poland and from the Lower Rhine, and women-folk whose only trade was with their tail, trulls the beadles had driven from the doors.

Here, too, the magicians and witch doctors who had escaped the scaffold had set up their wizards' kitchens; by the initiated, by Venetians and alchemists these unknown villages were reckoned among the sanctuaries of the black art. In Fortunio's hands I had seen a manuscript from the pen of Rabbi Nilufer – the same who, driven from Smyrna, had on his wanderings been a guest among the woods. In his writings one saw world history mirrored as in muddy pools on the banks of which water-rats nest. Here was to be found the key to many a murky intrigue: thus rumour ran that after his banishment from Perouard Master Villon had found shelter in one of these pinewood warrens, in which along with many another shady crew the Coquillards had made their base. Later they flitted over into Burgundy, but here they had always a haven of refuge.

Whatever elements from the outside world went underground in the forest multiplied ten- and a hundred-fold in its womb. This was the breeding-place of the mean huntsmen who offered themselves in house and field as destroyers of vermin – according to Nilufer, the Pied Piper of Hamelin had disappeared here with the children. But from the woods came too the dainty deceivers who appear with coach and lackeys and are to be found even at the courts of noble counts. Thus from the forest a strain of evil blood flowed into the veins of the world. Where there were killings or thuggery one of the shady crew was always by, nor were they missing from the minuets that poor devils dance on the gallows hill with the wind for partner.

To all these the Ranger was lord and master, to be kissed on the hem of his red hunting coat or on the calf of his boot when he sat in the saddle. For his part he dealt with them at his pleasure, and from time to time had a dozen or two strung up like scarecrows on the trees if they seemed to spawn too abundantly. Otherwise they might lodge and feast on his lands as they pleased.

As protector of the land of vagabonds the Ranger enjoyed in the world outside hidden and far-spread powers. Wherever the structures raised by the ordered life of man began to crumble, his brood sprang up like mushroom spawn. They swarmed and burrowed wherever retainers refused service to their hereditary masters, where crews mutinied on storm-tossed barks, where warrior kings were left deserted on stricken fields.

The Chief Ranger alone was well served by these powers. When he received the Mauretanians in his town house there surrounded him a swarm of henchmen – green-liveried huntsmen, red-coated lackeys in their black pumps, major-domos and confidants of all sorts. At such feasts could be felt something of the pleasant ease which the Ranger loved in his woods; the broad hall was warm and gleamed with lights – but the light was not that of the sun, but of flame and the glint of gold in dark caves.

Like a diamond gleaming out from the glowing dross of an alchemist's crucible, there grew up from time to time in the forest warrens women of surpassing beauty. Like all people of the woods, they were serfs of the Ranger, and on his travels they rode in litters in his train. When the young Mauretanians were his guests in the little houses before the town gates, and he was of a good humour, it would come about that he displayed his odalisques as others would their jewels. He would call them into the billiard-room where the company had collected to drink spiced wine after the heavy meal, and set out the balls for them to play. Then one would see in the red light of the lamps their unveiled bodies bowed over the green table bending slowly and turning in the movements of the game. In this connection there were tales from his woods that were grosser yet – of how after long chase after fox or bear he feasted on the sward surrounded by trophies of war and the chase, and sat in state on his high chair gory with slaughtered game.

Such women served him too as the finest of lures wherever he was busied in affairs of the world. All who drew near the treacherous blossoms which had sprung from the swamps fell under the spell that brings abasement in its train. In our Mauretanian time we saw many succumb to whom a great destiny had beckoned; for it is the lofty spirit that first becomes entangled in such weeds.

This was the stock destined to settle the land when the Ranger had won complete mastery over the Marina, like crab apple, wild poppy and henbane, replacing noble fruits in war-sacked gardens. Then instead of the giver of wine and bread the strange gods would be raised up – Diana for one, transformed in the marshes to a savage goddess of fertility, and hung about with grape-like clusters of golden breasts; along with her would come terrible idols which strike fear with claws, with horns and with tusks, and demand sacrifices unworthy of man.

13

That was how things stood in the seventh year after Alta Plana, and to that campaign we traced back the evils that cast their shadow over the land. It is true that we had both taken part in it and mixed in the mêlée at the entrance to the passes in the ranks of the Purple Horse, but we had done so only to discharge our bounden duty, which was to strike and not to grope after rights and wrongs. But since the right arm is more obedient than the heart, our spirit was with the people who defended their hereditary freedom so gallantly against great odds. In their victory we saw more than the fortune of arms.

Then, too, we had made hospitable friends in Alta Plana, for before the passes young Ansgar, the son of the Master of the Bodan Alps, had fallen into our hands and had exchanged gifts with us. From the terrace we saw the Bodan Alp in the far distance like a blue patch hidden deep in the sea of ice-clad peaks, and we drew a sense of security from the thought that in their valley home we would be received like brothers at any hour with bed and board.

After we had returned to our homeland far in the North and locked up our weapons again in the armoury, we had a mind to lead a life untouched by violence, and thought of our old studies. We reported to the Mauretanians for honourable discharge, and were entered in the roll of retired veterans with the right to wear the black, red and white ribbon. We would certainly not have lacked the courage and powers of judgement to climb to high rank in the order. But we had never acquired the faculty of looking down on the sufferings of the weak and anonymous like senators glancing down into the arena from their seats of privilege. But what is to be done if the weak deny the laws prescribed, and in their blindness pull back with their own hands the bars and bolts which have been put to for their protection? We could not, therefore, altogether criticize the Mauretanians, for right and unright were now ravelled together; men of firm courage tottered and the time was ripe for terror. In this respect man-made order is like the universe – from time to time it must plunge into the flames to be born anew.

We were right, therefore, to keep clear of affairs in which no honour was to be won, and to return peacefully to the Marina; there by the sunny banks we would devote ourselves to flowers, those fleeting coloured signals which in their secret painted script express the unchangeable order of things, and are like timepieces that never fail to tell the hour. But house and garden had scarcely been set in order and the work advanced so far that its first fruits were promised when the flames of arson began to flicker up from the Cam-

54

pagna behind the Marble Cliffs. When later the unrests laid hold upon the Marina we were compelled to keep ourselves informed, so as to be acquainted with the nature and extent of the threat.

In the Campagna dwelt old Belovar, who was often to be found in Lampusa's kitchen. He came with herbs and rare roots which his women-folk dug out from the rich earth of the pastures, and which Lampusa dried for her drinks and potions. Thus we had struck up a friendship and emptied many a can of beer with him on the bench which stood on the court before the kitchen. He could be trusted to know all the names the country-folk give to flowers, of which they can distinguish a great number; in order to enrich our glossary we willingly listened to his lore. He knew, too, the spots where rare varieties were to be found – the flower which blooms among the scrub and has a goat-like smell, the orchid with a lip shaped like a human body, and a rag-wort with flowers like panther's eyes. So it came about that we often asked for his company when we collected speci-mens behind the Marble Cliffs. There he knew every path and trail up to the edge of the forest; but, more important still, when the herdsmen were hostile, we found sure pro-tection in his company.

This aged man embodied the best that the pasture-lands had to offer – something quite different from the picture dreamt up by the mincing dandies who thought to have found the ideal man among the herdsmen and sang his praises in rose-water rhymes. Old Belovar was seventy years old, tall and spare, with a white beard that contrasted sharply with his black hair. Of his features his dark eyes were the most striking, sharp like falcon's, spying out the distance and embracing the whole landscape in their sweep; but when he was enraged they had a wolfish glint. In his ears he wore golden rings, round his head a red scarf, and round his waist a red girdle which left bare the pommel and point of his dagger. In the haft of this trusty weapon were cut eleven notches varnished over with dyer's red.

When we came to know him the old man had just taken

55

his third wife, a lass of sixteen years, whom he kept strictly in order and beat into the bargain when he was in his cups. If he came to speak of the blood feuds his eyes would light up, and we saw that so long as it beat the heart of the foe drew him like a mighty magnet. We saw, too, that the fame of his vendettas had made him a singer like many more in the Campagna. There when they drank by the fire to the honour of the herdsmen's gods it often happened that one would rise from the circle and in flowing words laud the mortal stroke with which he laid his enemy low.

With time we took to the old man and were glad to see him, just as one puts up with a faithful hound although the spirit of the wolf still glows within him. Even if in Belovar there blazed primitive fires, yet there was nothing ignoble in the man, and therefore he hated the powers of darkness that pushed forward out of the forest into the Campagna. We soon saw, too, that his rude spirit was not without virtues; in his trusty heart there burned a warmer flame than is known in towns. Thus to him friendship was no mere sentiment, but something which blazed as spontaneously and as fiercely as hate. We, too, had caught an inkling of this when Brother Otho, years before, had turned the tables in open court during a knotty case in which the consuls of the Marina had ensnared the old man. Then he began to take us to his heart, and even when he saw us from afar his eyes gleamed.

Soon we had to be on our guard not to utter a wish when he was near, for he would have wormed his way into the Griffon's nest and caught its young to give us joy. Like a trusty weapon that is never out of one's hand, he was at our disposal at any hour. In him we discovered the power we enjoy when a man gives himself to us body and soul, a power which dies out with the coming of an ordered way of life.

So through this friendship alone we felt that we were well shielded from the dangers which threatened from the Campagna. Many a night when we sat silent over our work in library and herbarium the flames of sacked houses would light up the edge of the cliffs. Often such incidents took place so close by that when the north wind blew the sounds were borne over to us. Then we heard the blows of the battering-ram pounding on the door of the courtyard, and the pitiful lowing of the cattle in their flaming byres. The wind carried across to us, too, the low hum of voices and the note of the bells sounding in the private chapels, and when all this died away we strained our ears long into the night.

But we knew that no ill threatened our Hermitage so long as the old herdsman and his wild tribe camped on the steppe.

14

On the other side of the cliffs towards the Marina the case was different; here we could count upon the support of a Christian monk, Father Lampros, from the cloister of Maria Lunaris, whom the people know and venerate as Our Lady of the Crescent. In these two men, herdsman and monk, there came to light that diversity which native soil produces in men no less than in plants. In the old avenger of blood feuds there lived the spirit of the pasture-lands, which have never been cut by the iron of a ploughshare; in the priest, that of the vineyard loam, which in the course of centuries and through the labour of man's hands has become as fine as the sand of an hourglass.

It was from Upsala that we had first heard of Father Lampros, and that through Ehrhardt, who was keeper of the herbarium there and supplied us with material for our work. At that time we were occupied with the study of plant formation – how they arrange their parts like radii within a circle, the way in which they form round an axis which is the basis of all organic patterns, and, lastly, how crystallization gives meaning to growth as the clock face does to the moving finger. Ehrhardt now informed us that we had living amongst us on the Marina the author of the magnificent work on the symmetry of fruits – Phyllobius, a name which hid the person of Father Lampros. This news awoke our curiosity, and, having written the monk a brief note, we visited him in the cloister of Our Lady of the Crescent.

The cloister lay so close by that from the Hermitage one could see the tip of its spire. The church was a place of pilgrimage, and the way ran through gentle meadows on which ancient trees bloomed so richly that scarcely a speck of green was visible through the white blossom. At this hour of the morning not a soul was to be seen in the gardens, through which there blew a cool wind from the sea, yet so potently did the blossom work upon the senses that we seemed to traverse magic gardens. Soon we saw the cloister lying before us on its hilltop site with its church smiling in its loveliness. Even from a distance we could hear the drone of the organ accompanying the hymn with which the pilgrims adored the icon.

As the porter led us through the church we, too, did reverence to the miraculous image. We saw the royal lady on a throne of clouds, her feet resting as on a stool on a thin crescent moon, its sickle fashioned like a face gazing earthwards. Thus divinity was pictured as power dominating over mutability; in this form she was honoured as the goddess who provides for and dispenses to mankind.

In the inner cloister we were received by the circulator, who led us into the library which was Father Lampros's charge. Here he spent the hours laid aside for work, and here, surrounded by tall folios, we often sat and talked. The first time that we stepped through its doors we saw the Father, who had just come in from the garden, standing in the quiet room with a spray of gladiolus in his hand. He still wore his wide-brimmed hat, and on his white cloak played the bright light which fell through the clerestory windows.

We found in him a man of some fifty years, moderate of stature and finely built. As we drew near to him fear laid hold on us, for the face and hands of this monk seemed to us unusual and disturbing. I might almost say that they appeared like those of a corpse, and it was difficult to believe that there was life-blood in them. They seemed to be modelled from soft wax with this effect, that the play of the features came only slowly to the surface and was more an illumination of the face than a movement of muscles. There was something very formal and symbolic, too, in the way he lifted his hand as he spoke – a favourite gesture. And yet this body had a delicate grace which seemed to have pervaded it like a breath animating a puppet. Nor did he lack joviality.

As we exchanged greetings, Brother Otho remarked in praise of the icon that in it he saw united on a higher plane the graces of Vesta and of Fortuna; thereupon the monk lowered his eyes to the ground with a courteous gesture and then raised them again with a smile. It seemed as if, after reflecting on it, he took the words as a votive offering.

From this and many other traits we learned that Father Lampros avoided argument; his silences were more effective than his words. So, too, in the science of which he was counted among the masters, he took no part in the squabbles of the schools. It was his firm belief that each theory in natural history represents a contribution towards genesis, for the human spirit in every age conceives the creation anew; in each interpretation lives no more truth than in a leaf that unfolds to fade. That was why he called himself – with that rare mixture of modesty and pride that marked his nature – Phyllobius, 'he who lives with the leaves'.

That Father Lampros did not willingly contradict was another sign of the courtesy which was so finely developed in his nature. Since at the same time he had the upper hand intellectually, he contrived to accept the speaker's words and return them to him with an expression of agreement which raised them to a higher plane. It was thus he returned the greeting of Brother Otho, and therein lay not only the goodness of spirit which the clergy acquire in the course of the years, and mature like a noble wine – there was courtliness, too, such as is bred in noble houses, and endows its offshoots with a second and more subtle nature. There was also an element of pride in it; for a ruling spirit has its own judgement and pays no heed to common opinion. It was said that Father Lampros sprang from an ancient Burgundian house, but of the past he never spoke. From his secular life he had retained a signet ring with a red cornelian, on which was cut a griffon's wing with under it as motto the words, 'I bide my time.' Therein, too, were betrayed the two poles of his nature – modesty and pride.

Soon we were frequent visitors to the cloister of Our Lady of the Crescent, and passed the time in garden or library. Thus our little Flora became far richer than before; for Father Lampros had been collecting for years by the Marina, and we never left him without a bundle of mounted specimens annotated in his own hand and each a tiny work of art. Our association with him was also favourable to our work on the axis pattern of flowers, for it means much for a project if from time to time one can weigh it up in the company of a good brain. In this connection we gained the impression that Father Lampros, unobtrusively and without in any way coveting a share in authorship, was taking part in our work. Not only did he possess a great knowledge of phenomena, but knew, too, how to communicate those supreme moments of experience in which the true meaning of our own work runs through us like a lightning flash.

One morning, for instance, he led us to a bank of flowers where the cloister gardener had been early at work hoeing; over one spot was spread a red cloth. He remarked that here he had spared from the hoe a plant that would delight our eyes; but when he withdrew the cloth we saw nothing more than a young growth of that type of plantain which Linnaeus called Majora, and which is to be found on every path that the foot of man ever trod. But when we bent down over it and scrutinized it carefully, it seemed to us of unusual size and regularity. Its circumference was a green circle divided off by the oval leaves which patterned the fringe with their points; in the centre rose in its brilliance the focal point of growth. It formed something as fresh and tender in its living tissues as it was indestructible in the genius of its symmetry. Then a shudder ran over us; we felt how closely united in us were the life wish and the death wish. When we raised ourselves up we looked into Father Lampros's smiling face. He had allowed us to partake of a mystery.

We had all the more reason to prize the moments of leisure which the Father set aside for us since his was a name revered among the Christians, and many sought him out in the hope of counsel and comfort. Yet he was also loved by those who put their faith in the twelve gods, and by the men from the North where the ancient deities are worshipped in spacious temples and thickets set apart. To them, too, when they visited him, he gave from the same source of strength, but no longer in priestly forms. Brother Otho, who knew many shrines and mysteries, often marked as the thing most to be wondered at in this spirit his ability to combine a high degree of knowledge with the observance of a strict rule. Brother Otho held that dogma accompanies spirituality in its successive stages of refinement: it is like a robe which during the ascent of the first steps is shot with gold and purples, but with each step acquires a quality which renders it invisible to our eyes, until gradually the pattern dissolves in light.

Because of the tribute of confidence paid to Father Lampros by all the forces at work on the Marina, the course of events there held no secrets from him. He had a clearer view of the game than any other, and thus it seemed strange to us that his monastic life was unaffected by it. Rather it appeared that his spirits rose and brightened with every step which brought the danger nearer.

We often discussed this over our fire of vine-cuttings in the Hermitage, for in times of threat such personalities tower above the weak herd. Sometimes we asked ourselves if to him ruin seemed already too far advanced for cure, or whether modesty and pride prevented him from joining in party strife with word or deed. But Brother Otho best summed up the situation by saying that, for such natures as his, destruction had no terrors, and that they were so constituted as to pass into the fiery furnace as if through the portals of their father's house. Of us all, perhaps he alone, deep in his dreams behind the cloister walls, was in complete contact with reality.

However that may be, if Father Lampros scorned his own safety he was constant in his solicitude on our account. Often notes would come, which he signed Phyllobius, advising us strongly to make an excursion to one spot or another to find a rare flower just then in bloom. Then we surmised that at a certain hour he wished to be sure that we were far away, and acted accordingly. Probably he chose this method since he learned much under inviolable seals. It struck us, too, that if we were not in residence at the Hermitage his messengers consigned these letters through Erio, but not through Lampusa.

15

When the tide of destruction raged more furiously round the Marble Cliffs memories awoke in us of our Mauretanian times, and we weighed up the possibility of a solution through force. On the Marina the rival powers were still so evenly balanced that a small force would tip the scales; for so long as the clans fought among themselves and Biedenhorn held back undecided with his mercenaries, the Chief Ranger had only insignificant numbers at his disposal.

We pondered whether to give chase to the huntsmen by night with Belovar and his tribe, and to string up the torn bodies of each one that fell into our net at the cross-roads; thus we would speak to the knaves from the forest villages in the only speech they understood. When we drew up such plans the old warrior made his broad falchion leap in its sheath for joy and pressed us to whet the hunting spears and starve the hounds until their red tongues lolled to the ground at the scent of blood. Then we too felt the power of the instinct run through our limbs like a flash.

But when we discussed the situation more thoroughly in the herbarium or library our decision was strengthened to resist with spiritual forces alone. After Alta Plana we had discovered – so we believed – that there are weapons stronger than those which cut or stab; yet from time to time, like children, we fell back on that earlier world in which terror rules supreme. We did not yet know the full measure of man's power.

In this respect our commerce with Father Lampros was most valuable to us. No doubt our own hearts would have led us to a decision in accordance with the state of mind in which we had returned to the Marina; yet at such turning-points in our life a third person aids us. The presence of a good master reveals to us our true desires and enables us to be ourselves. His noble image lives deep in our heart because in him we first discern that of which we are capable.

Thus a strange period began for us by the Marina. While evil flourished like mushroom spawn in rotten wood, we plunged deeper into the mystery of flowers, and their chalices seemed larger and more brilliant than before. But, above all, we continued our study of language, for in the word we recognized the gleaming magic blade before which tyrants pale. There is a trinity of word, liberty and spirit.

I can claim that our work prospered. Many a morning we woke in high spirits and savoured on our tongues the clean taste that accompanies perfect health. Then we would find no difficulty in putting names to things, and moved about in the Hermitage as if its rooms were magnetically charged. As we passed through the apartments and the garden we felt a slight headiness and exaltation, and from time to time we laid our leaves of notes upon the chimney.

On such days when the sun stood high we would make our way to the summit of the Marble Cliffs. Stepping over the dark hieroglyphs of the lance-head vipers on the snake-path, we began to ascend the bright gleaming steps of the rock staircase. From the highest peak of the cliffs, which rose dazzling in the midday sun and cast its brilliance to distant horizons, we looked long upon the land and sought out some sign of its salvation in every ridge and fold. Then the scales seemed to fall from our eyes, and we caught something of its imperishable splendour, which lived on like an image in poetry. It was with joy that we felt the certainty come over us that destruction finds no place in the elements, and that its seeming power moves on the surface of life like a swirling ghostly mist which cannot withstand the sun.

And we felt: if only we could live in the indestructible cells, we would pass freely through every phase of destruction as if through an open door leading from one hall of state to others yet more magnificent.

Often, when we stood on the summit of the Marble Cliffs, Brother Otho would say that this was the true meaning of life – to recapitulate creation in what is ephemeral, like the child imitating in play his father's work. This, he held, gave meaning to seed and begetting, to building and ordered life, to image and poetry – that in them the master work reveals itself as if in a mirror of many-coloured glass which soon must break.

16

So we think back with pleasure to our days of pride. But we must not pass over in silence those others during which dejection had the upper hand. In our hours of weakness destruction appears to us in terrifying forms, like the images one sees in the temples of the Furies.

Therefore there dawned for us many a grey morning on which we wandered aimlessly through the Hermitage and mournfully meditated in herbarium and library. Then we would make to the shutters and read by lamplight yellowed documents and manuscripts which once had been our companions on our constant travels. We opened old letters and turned over the pages of treasured books in search of comfort – books which still diffused the warmth of hearts long turned to dust. In the same way the glow of earthly summers lives on in dark veins of coal.

On days like these, when depression held sway, we shut even the doors leading to the garden, for the fresh scent of the flowers was too strong for our senses. In the evening we would send little Erio to the rock kitchen so that Lampusa might draw for him a jug of the wine that dates its vintage from the year of the comet.

Then when the fire of vine-cuttings blazed on the hearth we brought out the scent amphorae in accordance with a custom we had adopted in Britain. It was our wont to collect for them the flower petals in their seasons, and once we had dried them to press them into wide-bellied jars. In winter when we raised the coverings of the vessels the bright flowers had long since lost their colour and faded to the shade of time-yellowed silk and pale purple stuffs. But from this flowery aftermath there rose a wonderful perfume like the memory of mignonette and rose gardens.

For these mournful feasts, too, we burned heavy tapers of bees' wax. They were the remainder of the parting gift from Deodat, the Provençal knight, who had fallen long since in the wild Taurus. By their shimmer we thought of that noble friend and of the evening hours we had talked away with him on the high walls of Rhodes while the sun went down in the cloudless Aegean sky. As it sank, a gentle breath of air was wafted up from the galley harbour to the town. The sweet scent of the roses mixed with the aroma of the fig-trees, and in the sea breeze there mingled the essence of distant wood- and shrub-clad slopes. But stronger than all, a rich, exquisite perfume mounted from the earthworks in which camomile blossomed in soft yellow masses.

With the scent rose the last honeyladen bees which flew through loophole and embrasure to find the hives in the little gardens. So often had their drunken humming delighted us as we stood on the rampart of the Porta d'Amboise that, when we parted, Deodat gave us a supply of their wax to carry with us on our journey, 'so that you

65

may not forget the hum of the golden bees on the rose-grown island'. And, indeed, when we burned the candles there came from their wicks a delicate aromatic scent of spices and of the flowers that bloom in the gardens of the Saracens.

Then we emptied our glasses to old and distant friends and to the lands of this world. When the winds of death are abroad there is no denying that fear lays hold on us. Then we wonder over our food and drink how much longer a place will be laid for us at table. For the earth is fair.

In addition, a thought weighed heavily upon us which always runs in the heads of men whose labours are on works of the spirit. We had spent not a few years on the study of plants and had spared neither oil nor pains. Ungrudgingly we had staked on it what we had inherited from our father. Now the first ripe fruits were falling into our laps. For there were the letters, the papers, the notebooks and collections of flowers, the diaries of war years and years of travel, and, above all, the material on language which we had gathered together from many thousands of little fragments – stones in a mosaic of which the construction was already far advanced. Of these manuscripts we had up to now published only a small portion, for Brother Otho held that casting pearls was misspent labour. We were living in times during which the author is condemned to solitude. Yet, even so, there was much we would gladly have seen printed – not for the sake of the fame, which is one aspect of illusion no less than the passing minute, but because print bears the seal of finality and immutability, the sight of which rejoices even the lonely heart. It is easier to depart when things are in order.

When fearful over the fate of our papers we often thought of Phyllobius and his good-humoured serenity. But we led a different life, and one that was lived in the world. To us it seemed unbearably hard that we should have to part from the work into which we had spun something of ourselves, which was the soil of our roots. To comfort us, however, we had the mirror of Nigromontanus, which always cheered us when we looked at it in such a mood. It was part of the legacy of my old master and had this property, that through it the rays of the sun were concentrated into an intense fire. Things set aflame by such ardour passed into incorruptibility in a manner of which Nigromontanus said that it was comparable only to the purest distillation. He had learned this art in the cloisters of the Far East, where the treasures of the dead are burned to be their eternal retinue. In the same way he held that anything kindled with the aid of this mirror was preserved in the invisible more surely than behind doors of armour. It was carried over by a flame which gave forth neither smoke nor drossy glow into realms that lie beyond destruction. This Nigromontanus called the haven of annihilation, and we resolved to seek it when the hour of ruin had come.

Therefore we prized the mirror as a key to lofty halls, and on such evenings would cautiously open the blue case which enclosed it to rejoice in its sparkling. Then its disc of limpid rock-crystal framed with an amber ring glanced in the light of the candles. In this setting Nigromontanus had engraved a motto in sun runes which was worthy of his daring spirit:

> Even should the earth burst like a cannon-shot,
> Yet will our passing be in fire and white-hot glow.

On the reverse were scratched in slender Pali script the names of three royal widows who at the rites of the dead had mounted the funeral pyre which Brahmins had set alight with the aid of this same mirror.

Beside the mirror lay another little lamp, also cut from rock-crystal and bearing the sign of Vesta. Its purpose was to conserve the power of the fire for sunless hours or for moments which demanded haste. It was with this lamp and not with torches that the pyre was set alight beside Olympus when Peregrinus Proteus, later called Phoenix, sprang into the blaze before a mighty throng of people in order to make himself one with the ether. The world knows of this man and of his lofty deed only through the lying and distorted account of Lucian.

Every good weapon has magic qualities; by merely looking at it we feel ourselves wonderfully strengthened. So it was with us and the mirror of Nigromontanus: its radiance foretold to us that we would not perish entirely; rather that the best in us was inaccessible to the lower powers. Thus our highest gifts rest like eagles unassailable in their eyries among the crystal air.

Father Lampros, it is true, would smile and say that there are sarcophagi for the spirit as well. The hour of destruction, he held, should, on the contrary, be the hour of fullest life. A priest could speak thus who felt himself drawn by death as if by far cataracts which catch the rainbows in their whirl of spray. But we were in the prime of life and felt sorely in need of signs which even the human eye can recognize. For us mortals the true and invisible light shines out only in the multiple hues of the rainbow.

17

It struck us that the days on which we were a prey to low spirits were also days of mist, during which the countryside lost its smiling look. Then the wreaths rose from the forests like steam from witches' cauldrons and rolled forward over the Campagna in thick banks. They piled up against the Marble Cliffs and, when the sun rose, pushed lazy wisps down into the valley until soon the tops of the spires had disappeared under the white vapour.

In such weather we felt ourselves robbed of our powers of sight, and sensed evil stealing over the land as if under a thick cloak. Therefore we did well to pass the day at home by candlelight and over wine; and yet often an urge came on us to go out. For we felt that not only did the 'glow-worms' ply their trade out there, but that somehow the country was at the same time changing its form, as if its reality were diminishing. Therefore on misty days we often resolved to make an excursion, and in that case sought out the pasture-lands in particular. There was always, too, some special plant which we aimed to add to our spoils. We sought, if I may say so, to keep fast hold, in the midst of chaos, on Linnaeus's masterpiece which represents one of the watch-towers from which the mind surveys the territory of untamed growth. In this sense the plucking of a tiny plant brought us great illumination.

Mingled with this there was something else which might be described as a sense of shame – that we did not regard the woodland breed as enemies. That is, we always maintained that we were on the track of plants and not on the warpath, and had therefore to avoid base forms of evil as one goes out of the way of swamps and wild animals. We did not attribute to the Lemur folk freedom of will. Such powers must never be allowed to dictate the law to us to such an extent that we lose sight of truth.

On such days the steps of the stairs leading up to the Marble Cliffs were damp with mist, and cool winds drove the wreaths of mist down over them. Although much had altered in the pasture-land, the old paths were still familiar to us. They led through the ruins of rich farms about which there now hung the smell of burnt-out fires. In the ruined stalls we saw whitening the bones of the cattle, with here and there a hoof or horn and the chain still round the beast's neck. In the inner yard were piled the household goods as the 'glow-worms' had thrown them from the windows before ransacking them. There lay the broken cradle between chair and table, and round them rose the green nettles. Only seldom did we stumble on scattered groups of herdsmen driving a few cattle, and these mere runts. Infectious airs had risen from the corpses rotting on the pastures and caused the herds to die off in large numbers. Thus the decline of order brings good fortune to none.

After an hour we came to old Belovar's farm, which was almost the only one to call up memories of old times, for it lay there rich in cattle and undamaged in its circle of green meadows. The reason was that old Belovar was both free herdsman and clan chief, and that from the beginning of the troubles he had kept his property free of all roaming rabble; therefore for long no huntsman or 'glow-worm' had ventured to pass by even in the distance. Those of them he had laid low in open country or in the brushwood he counted among his good works, and therefore did not even cut a new notch in his dagger. He also insisted strictly that all cattle which perished on his grounds should be buried deep and covered with lime. So it came about that the way to him took one through great herds of red and dappled cattle, and that his house and barns stood out fresh and bright from afar. The little gods, too, who guarded his bounds always laughed at us with the gleam of newly brought offerings.

So at times in war an outerwork will remain intact when the keep has long since fallen. In this fashion the old man's farm offered us a sort of centre of support. Here we could rest and chat with him in safety while Milina, his young wife, prepared for us in the kitchen wine with saffron or set butter scones to bake. Then, too, the old man still had a mother, who was almost a hundred years old and yet went through house and courtyard as upright as a wand. We liked to speak with the old dame, for she was well versed in plants and knew sayings of such force as made the blood run cold. And we had her lay her hands upon us when we said farewell to go farther on our way.

Generally the old man wanted to accompany us, but we were loath to have him with us. It seemed as if his presence drew the woodsmen from the forest villages upon us just as the dogs stir when the wolf roams round the outhouses. That was certainly after the old man's heart; but we had other things in mind. We went without weapons, without followers, and drew over us light silver-grey cloaks to be the better hid in the mist. In this wise we groped our way cautiously forward through marsh and reeds towards the horn-shaped thickets and the edge of the forest.

Very soon, when we left the pastures, we marked that the

70

feeling of violence was drawing closer and growing stronger. The mist rolled in waves in the undergrowth and the reeds whistled in the wind. Even the very ground under our feet struck us as stranger and less familiar. But most disquieting of all was that our memory strayed. Then the landscape became utterly treacherous and vague and like the country one sees in dreams. Thus there were always spots which we recognized with certainty, but hard by them rose, like islands emerging from the sea, new and mysterious territories. To make out their true and accurate topography we required all our energies. We therefore did well to avoid the adventures after which old Belovar so thirsted.

In this way we would walk and pass the hours in the marsh- and reed-lands. If I do not describe the details of our work it is because we were bruised with things which lie beyond speech and which therefore elude the spell that words exert. But everyone will remember how his mind has laboured in regions which he cannot portray, whether it were in dreams or in deep thought. It seemed as if he were groping for the right road in labyrinths or sought to unravel the figures among the patterns of an optical illusion. And often he awoke wonderfully strengthened. That is where our best work takes place, and so it seemed to us, too, that in our struggle speech was still inadequate, and that we must penetrate into the depths of the dream if we were to withstand the threat against us.

And when we stood alone among the swamps and reeds the enterprise appeared to us like a fine game in which each stroke calls forth its parry. Then the mists rolled up denser than before, and yet at the same time there seemed to grow within us the strength which creates order.

18

Yet on none of these expeditions did we neglect the flowers. They told us our direction like a compass piloting through unknown seas. Such was the case on that day when we penetrated to the heart of the Flayer's Copse, one which we later remembered only with horror.

In the morning when we saw the mists rising from the forests up to the Marble Cliffs we had decided to go in search of a red woodland orchid, and once Lampusa had provided breakfast we soon set out on our way. This red orchid is a flower which grows alone in woods and thickets and bears the name 'rubra', which Linnaeus gave it, to distinguish it from two paler species; yet it is rarer than either of these. Since this plant loves spots where the thick wood thins to a glade, Brother Otho held that it was perhaps best to be sought at Köppels-Bleek. Thus the herdsmen called an old clearing which was said to lie at the point where the sickle-shaped Flayer's Copse joins the edge of the forest – a place of ill repute.

At midday we were with old Belovar, but because we felt the need of all our spiritual powers we did not sup there. We drew the silver-grey cloaks over us, and since the old dame had laid hands upon us without finding cause to stay us, the old man parted with us reassured.

Immediately we had crossed his bounds a wild driving mist set in which blotted out all shapes and forms and soon led us astray. Thus we wandered in a circle in moss and moor, halting now and then among groups of old willows or beside turbid pools out of which the sedge grew high.

On this day the desolate scene seemed to have more life in it, for in the mist we heard calls and thought to catch sight of figures passing close by us in the fog, but without seeing us. In this confusion we would certainly have missed the way to Flayer's Copse, but we stuck close to the sundew. We knew that this plant had settled in the moist zone which ringed the woods, and followed the pattern of its shining green and red-haired leaves like the fringe of a carpet. In this way we reached the three tall poplars which in clear weather stood out like lance-shafts marking the tip of the Flayer's Copse. From this point we groped along the sickle-shaped edge of the thicket up to the edge of the forest, and there pushed into the Flayer's Copse at its broadest point.

Once we had broken through a thick hedge of dogwood and blackthorn we entered the high forest, territory where the blow of an axe had never resounded. The ancient trunks, the pride of the Chief Ranger, stood gleaming damp like pillars with their capitals hidden by the mist. We walked among them as if through a spacious hall, and, like the magic setting of a stage, festoons of ivy and clematis blooms hung down towards us out of the void. The ground was piled high with mould and rotting branches, in the bark of which fiery red mushrooms had sprung up, so that we felt for a moment like divers wandering among coral gardens. Wherever one of the mighty trunks had fallen from age or been struck by lightning, we stepped out on to a little clearing on which the yellow foxglove grew in thick clumps. On the rotting ground the deadly nightshade bloomed in pro-fusion; on its stalks the dark purple calices shook like funeral bells.

The air was still and oppressive, and yet we put up birds of all kinds. We heard, for instance, the fine chirping with which the woodcock slips through the larches, and the warn-ing call with which the startled thrush interrupts its song. Chuckling, the wryneck hid in a hollow alder stem, and in the elm-tops an oriole accompanied us with its clownish laughter. In the distance we heard the drunken cooing of the wood-pigeons and the hammering of the woodpeckers on the dead wood.

We were slowly breasting a gentle rise when Brother Otho, who was slightly ahead, called back to me that the clearing was quite near. This was the moment when I saw the orchid we sought shimmering in the dusk and hastened

73

towards it with joy. The flower nestled closely in the copper-brown beech leaves like a woodland bird. I saw its slender leaves and the dark red blossom with the pale tip to the petals that is its distinguishing mark.

When a collector comes suddenly upon a plant or animal a feeling of joy comes over him, as if nature had bestowed on him a precious gift. On making such a find I used to call Brother Otho before touching it, so that he might share the joy with me, but just as I was about to raise my eyes towards him I heard a groan which startled me with fear. It was the noise with which the breath of life slowly leaves our breasts when we are mortally wounded. I saw him standing before me on the crest of the slope as if spellbound, and when I hastened to him he raised his hand to show where I should look. Then I felt as if cruel talons had laid hold upon my heart, for before me lay the abode of tyranny in all its shame.

19

We stood behind a small bush which bore flame-red berries and looked out on to the clearing of Köppels-Bleek. The weather had changed, for here we could see no trace of the wreaths of mist which had accompanied us since we left the Marble Cliffs. On the contrary, things stood out in full definition, as if in the centre of a cyclone, in still and unstirred air. The voices of the birds, too, were silent, and only a cuckoo flickered to and fro, as is the wont of his kind, on the dark edge of the wood. Now near, now far, we heard his mocking and questioning laughter call 'Cuckoo, Cuckoo,' and then descend in a triumphant cadenza which made an icy chill run through our blood.

The clearing was overgrown with withered grass which only in the background gave way to the grey teasel which one finds on felling sites. From this parched base two large bushes, which at first glance we took for laurels, rose strangely fresh; yet their leaves were flecked with the yellow to be seen on butchers' stalls. They grew on either side of an old barn with yawning doors which stood in the clearing. The light which played upon it was unlike any light of the sun, but was hard and shadowless, so that the whitewashed building stood out sharply defined. At intervals the walls were divided off by black beams with tripod bases, and over them rose to a point a grey shingle-roof. Against them, too, leaned stakes and hooks.

Over the dark door on the gable-end a skull was nailed fast, showing its teeth and seeming to invite entry with its grin. Like a jewel in its chain, it was the central link of a narrow gable frieze which appeared to be formed of brown spiders. Suddenly we guessed that it was fashioned of human hands fastened to the wall. So clearly did we see this that we picked out the little peg driven through the palm of each one.

On the trees, too, which ringed the clearing, bleached the death's-heads; many a one with eye sockets already moss-grown seemed to scan us with a dark smile. Except for the mad dance in which the cuckoo flitted round the whiteness of the skulls it was absolutely still. I heard Brother Otho whisper half in a dream: 'Yes, this is Köppels-Bleek.'

The interior of the barn lay almost in darkness, and we could distinguish only, close to the entrance, a flaying bench on which a skin was stretched out. Behind it other pale fungoid shapes shimmered out of the dark background. Towards them, as if into a hive, we saw buzzing swarms of steel-coloured and golden flies. Then the shadow of a great bird fell over the spot. Its movements were those of a vulture which swooped down on the teasel field on jagged wings. Only when we saw it rooting with its beak and sinking its red neck into the upturned soil did we become aware that a dwarf was working there with a pick, and that the bird followed his handiwork like a raven behind the plough.

Now the dwarf laid down his pick and, whistling an air, walked over to the barn. He was clad in a grey jerkin, and we saw that he rubbed his hands as if after work well done. When he had entered the barn there began a pounding and scraping on the flaying bench; he whistled his air throughout in elfish merriment. Then we heard the wind rocking itself as if in accompaniment among the pines so that the pale skulls on the trees rattled in chorus. Into its lament was mixed the swaying of the hooks and the twitching of the withered hands on the barn wall. The noise was that of wood and bone, like a puppet show in the kingdom of the dead. At the same time there bore down upon the wind a clinging heavy and sweet smell of corruption, which made us shiver to the marrow of our bones. Within us we felt the melody of life touch its darkest and deepest chord.

Later we were unable to say how long we had watched the goblin figure – perhaps no longer than a second. Then we seemed to waken and, seizing each other's hands, we rushed back into the high wood of the Flayer's Copse, accompanied by the mocking call of the cuckoo. Now we knew the hell kitchen from which the mist drifted over the Marina – since we were determined not to give way, the old man of the forest had shown us it a little more clearly. Such are the dungeons above which rise the proud castles of the tyrants, and from them is to be seen rising the curling savoury smoke of their banquets. They are terrible noisome pits in which a God-forsaken crew revels to all eternity in the degradation of human dignity and human freedom. In such times the muses are silent, and truth begins to flicker like a torch in a current of foul air. Scarcely have the first mists begun to brew up than one sees the weak already giving ground, and even the warrior caste begins to lose heart when they see the masklike faces rising up to the battlements from the depths. So it comes about that in this world soldier's courage takes second place, and only the noblest spirits in our midst penetrate into the dwelling-place of terror. They know that all these images in reality live only in our hearts, and pass through them into the portals of victory as if they were mere mirrored shadows. Thus the masked terrors confirm them in their own reality.

But as for us, the dance of death on Köppels-Bleek had terrified us to the core, and it was with a shudder that we stood in the depth of the wood and listened to the cuckoo's call. But then shame came over us, and it was Brother Otho who insisted that we should at once return again to the clearing, because the little red flower had not been entered in our field-book. For it was our habit to enter all our finds in the journal on the spot, since we had learned that many things slipped our memory. So we may say with justice that our Florula Marinae grew in the field.

We therefore pushed forward again, without turning when the cuckoo called, as far as the little hill, and then sought out the plant among the fallen leaves. After we had once more looked at it well, Brother Otho dug it out by the roots with our spade. Then we measured the plant in all its parts with the compass, and along with the date entered in our little book the particulars of the place where the find had been made.

We men when we are busied about our appointed tasks fulfil an office; and it is strange how immediately we are possessed by a stronger feeling of invulnerability. We had experienced this already on the field of battle where the soldier, when the proximity of the enemy threatens to sap his courage, turns with a will to duties which his rank prescribes. There is great strength in the sight of the eyes when in full consciousness and unshaded by obscurities it is turned upon the things around us. In particular it draws nourishment from created things, and herein alone lies the power of science. Therefore we felt that even the tender flower in its imperishable pattern and living form strengthened us to withstand the breath of corruption.

Later when we made our way through the high forest to the edge of the wood the sun had come out, as it sometimes does before its setting on days of mist. A golden glow lay in the gaps among the crowns of the giant trees, and the moss, too, under our feet had a golden gleam. The call of the cuckoo had long since died away, but in the topmost withered twigs the nightingales had taken up their perch unseen – the fine singers whose voices filled the cool, fresh air. Then with a cavernous shimmer of green light the evening spread over the sky. A heavy scent streamed from the sprays of honeysuckle dangling from above, and with a hum of wings the gnats rose to their yellow horned blossoms. We saw them trembling gently and seemingly lost in a voluptuous dream before the erected flowers, and then with a vibration they thrust their slender, slightly curved tongue into the honeyed depths.

When we left the Flayer's Copse at the three poplars the pale sickle of the moon was already beginning to take on a golden hue and the stars stood out in the sky. In the sedgeland we came upon old Belovar, who had set out on our trail in the dusk with his servants and trackers. The old man laughed when later, over the saffron wine, we showed him the red flower which we had made our prize at Köppels-Bleek; but we were silent, and when we took our leave bade him look to his fair and undamaged farmstead.

20

There are certain experiences which force us to the test anew; for us one such was the glimpse into the flaying-hut at Köppels-Bleek. Our immediate resolve was to seek out Father Lampros, but before we were able to reach the monastery of Our Lady of the Crescent the catastrophe had already broken over us.

The next day we spent long over the arranging of manuscripts in the herbarium and library, and laid much in order for destruction by fire. Then, as darkness began, I once more sat for a short time in the garden on the terrace wall to enjoy the scent of the flowers. The warmth of the sun still lay over the beds, and yet the first cool was already rising from the grass of the river banks and laying the smell of the dust. Then the breath of night-scented stocks and evening primroses fell cascading down from the Marble Cliffs into the garden of the Rue-Garden Hermitage. And since there are scents which fall and others which rise, so a faint and subtle aroma mounted up through these heavy waves.

I traced it down and saw that the great gold-striped lily from Zipangu had opened in the dusk. It was still light enough to see the flame-shaped streak of gold and the brown tiger markings, too, which imposed their splendour on the white bloom. In its shining white setting the pistil stood out like the tongue of a bell, with the six slender stamens set around it in a circle. They were coated with brown pollen like the quintessence of opium, and as yet untouched by wing of butterfly, so that the delicate sheath shone in their midst. I bent over them and saw that their filaments still trembled like chords in an instrument of nature's making, a carillon from which there streamed, not harmonies, but a musk-scented essence. It will always remain a marvel that such delicate forms of life are imbued with so much passion.

While I was contemplating the lily thus a fine blue ray of light flashed on the road through the vineyards and advanced gropingly up the grape-clad hill. Then below I heard a vehicle stop before the Hermitage gates. Although we were expecting no guests, I hastened down to the door, mindful of the vipers, and saw standing there a powerful car humming softly like an almost imperceptibly vibrating insect. It bore the colours reserved for the high nobility of New Burgundy, and beside it stood two men of whom one gave the sign with which the Mauretanians recognize each other after dark. He told me his name, Braquemart, one which I remembered, and presented me then to the other, the young Prince of Sunmyra, a noble lord of New Burgundian stock.

I invited them to enter the Rue-Garden Hermitage and took them by the hand to guide them. So we walked three abreast up the snake-path in the failing light, and I remarked that the Count scarcely noticed the beasts, whereas Braquemart stepped out of their way with a mixture of scorn and circumspection.

We entered the library and there met Brother Otho, and while Lampusa laid out wine and baked meats we fell into conversation with our guests. Braquemart we knew from earlier days, but we had seen him only fleetingly, for he was often on his travels. He was a small, dark, haggard fellow whom we found somewhat coarse-grained, but, like all the Mauretanians, not without wit. He belonged to the race of men whom we jokingly called tiger hunters because they are usually to be met in the course of adventures of an exotic nature. He sought out danger in the way that others climb creviced rock-faces for sport: the plains he hated. He had that kind of stout heart which does not quail at obstacles, but unfortunately this virtue was coupled with contempt. Like all who hunger after power and mastery, he was led astray by his wild dreams into the realm of Utopias. It was his opinion that from the beginning of history there have been two races of men on this earth – the masters and the slaves – and that in the course of time the breeds had crossed. In this respect he was a pupil of old Pulverkopf, and, like him, demanded that they should be separated anew. Then, too, like every crude theoretician, he lived on the science of the moment and occupied himself with archaeology in particular. He was not subtle enough to sense that our spade infallibly turns up all the evidence which already existed in our minds, and, like many others before him, he had in this way discovered the cradle of the human race. We took part in the assembly before which he made his report on these excavations, and heard how in a distant desert he had stumbled on a fantastic tableland. There high crags of porphyry rose out of the wide plain; they had withstood the action of the weather and stood firm like bastions or rock islands. These Braquemart had scaled, and on their plateaux had discovered ruins of princes' palaces and temples of the sun. After describing their dimensions and characteristics, he called up a picture of the land. He showed us the rich green pastures, settled as far as the eye could see by herdsmen and peasants with their flocks, and above them on the towers of porphyry among the imperial splendour of their eyries the pristine rulers of the world. He set the ships sailing again with their purple poops down a river whose waters had long since dried up; one saw a hundred oars dip in the water with steady beat, like insect legs, and heard the clangour of the gongs and the lash falling on the backs of the unhappy galley slaves. These were images after his own heart. He belonged to the race of men who dream concretely – a very dangerous breed.

The young Prince also seemed remote and absent-minded, but after quite another fashion. He cannot have been much more than twenty, yet an air of deep suffering presented a strange contrast to his age. Although tall in stature, he bore himself with curved shoulders as if his height incommoded him. Nor did he seem to follow the drift of our talk. I had the impression that great age and extreme youth had met in his person – the age of his race and the youth of his body. Thus his whole being bore the deep stamp of decadence; one could see two forces at work in him – that of hereditary greatness and the contrary influence which the soil exerts upon all heredity. For heredity is dead men's riches.

It is true that I had expected the nobility to come forward in the last phase of the struggle for possession of the Marina. I had believed that one day they would rise in arms from their castles and keeps to be chivalrous leaders in the fight for freedom. Instead of which I saw this man old before his time, himself in need of support; the sight made it abundantly clear to me how far decay had gone. And yet it seemed a thing to wonder at that this weary dreamer felt himself called upon to give protection to others – in this way the weakest and purest take upon themselves the iron tasks of this earth.

Down below in front of the door I had already had an inkling of what brought this pair to us with dimmed lights, and Brother Otho seemed to know it, too, before even a word had been spoken. Then Braquemart asked us for a sketch of the situation, which Brother Otho presented in detail. The way in which Braquemart followed the story made it evident that he was extremely well informed on all the forces at play. He had already spoken with Biedenhorn, too, but with Father Lampros he was not acquainted.

The Prince, on the other hand, remained bowed in an attitude of reverie. Even the mention of Köppels-Bleek, which put Braquemart in a good temper, seemed to pass over his head; only when he heard of the prostitution of the ebernum did he start in anger from his seat. Then Brother Otho indicated in general terms our opinion of things and the way we must conduct ourselves. Braquemart heard him with courtesy, it is true, but at the same time with ill-concealed irony. One could read from his brow that he considered us merely as feeble visionaries, and that his own mind was made up. Thus there are situations in which each thinks the other a dreamer.

It may seem noteworthy that in this affair Braquemart wished to confront the Ranger, although there was much in common in their ways of thought and action. But it is an error which often runs through our thoughts that we deduce identity of goals from identity of methods, and conclude that the aims are the same. Yet there was a difference to this degree, that the Ranger had in mind to people the Marina with wild beasts, while Braquemart looked on it as land to be settled with slaves and their overlords. At bottom the question revolved round one of the internal conflicts between Mauretanians which it is not practicable to describe here. It is sufficient to indicate that between full-blown nihilism and unbridled anarchy there is a profound difference. Whether the abodes of men shall become desert or primeval forest depends upon the outcome of this struggle.

As far as Braquemart is concerned, he bore the unmistakable stamp of nihilism in its later stages. His was a cold, rootless intelligence, and with it went a leaning to Utopias. Then, too, like all his kind, he conceived of life as the mechanism of a clock, and therefore in force and terror he saw the gears which drive the timepiece of life. At the same time he indulged in the idea of a second artificial natural order, intoxicated himself with the perfume of synthetic flowers and the pleasures of mimed sensuality. Creation had died in his heart, and he had reconstructed it like a mechanical toy. The flowers which blossomed on his brow were blooms of ice. On seeing him one could not but think of his master's profound utterance: 'The desert is spreading; woe to him who within himself conceals a desert.'

And yet we felt slightly attracted to Braquemart – not so much because he had a stout heart, for the more stone-like a man becomes merit based on courage diminishes. What was attractive in him was rather a subtle air of suffering, the bitterness of a man who is sick at heart. He sought to wreak vengeance for it on the world, like a child laying waste a carpet of flowers in futile rage. Nor did he spare himself, but penetrated with cool daring into the labyrinths of fear. In the same way, when we have lost feeling for our homeland, we seek out the distant worlds of adventure.

In his thinking he took life for his model, and was insistent that thoughts should be armed with tooth and claw. Yet his theories were like the products of distillation, and in the process the true vital force was lost; they lacked a precious ingredient – the rich abundance which alone imparts a savour. The dominant quality of his plans was aridness, although there was no error to be found in his logic. Similarly, the trueness of a bell is lost through an invisible fault in the casting. The reason was that with him power was too much a matter of the intellect, and found too little expression in *grandezza*, in native *désinvolture*. In this respect the Chief Ranger had the better of him, for he wore his power like a good old hunting jacket that fitted him the better the oftener it was steeped in mire and blood. For this reason I had the impression that Braquemart was about to embark upon an ill-fated venture; in such encounters the theorist has always been worsted by the man of action.

It seemed that Braquemart had an inkling of his weakness with regard to the Chief Ranger, and for that reason had brought the young Prince with him. Yet to us it seemed that the latter was motivated by quite other interests; in this way there often spring up strange comradeships. Perhaps it was the Prince who was using Braquemart to ferry him to a distant shore. In that weak body there lived a strong urge towards suffering, and by it he was guided like a sleepwalker, without conscious thought, yet never losing the path. In the same way, on the field of battle, the good soldiers tear themselves from the ground with their last breath when the bugle sounds for the assault.

With Brother Otho I often thought back to this conversation, which took place under an unlucky star. The Prince spoke scarcely a word, and Braquemart displayed the unbearable air of superiority by which one may recognize the technician. We could read in his face that he inwardly made merry over our timidity, and without letting drop a single word about his own plans questioned us on the lie of the forests and pasture-lands. He also showed great interest in details about Fortunio's adventure and ill-fated end. From his questions we saw that he was planning a reconnaissance or operation in these parts, and suspected that, like an unskilled doctor, he would aggravate the evil. For it was, after all, no mere chance or adventure that had begun to bring forth the Ranger and his Lemur people from the darkness of the woods, and led them to deploy and show their real nature. Formerly rabble of this sort had been dealt with like common petty thieves, and their growing strength pointed to deep changes in the ordered relations, the health and well-being of the people. Now battle had to be joined, and therefore men were needed to restore a new order, and new theologians as well, to whom the evil was manifest from its outward phenomena down to its most subtle roots; then the time would come for the first stroke of the consecrated sword, piercing the darkness like a lightning flash. For this reason individuals had the duty of living in alliance with others, gathering the treasure of a new rule of law; but the alliance had to be stronger than before, and they more conscious of it. Thus even to win a brief race one lives according to a rule. But in this case there were at stake life in its highest form, liberty and the dignity of man. Braquemart, it is true, since he intended to pay the Ranger in his own coin, considered that such plans were mere flummeries. He had lost his own self-respect; from that loss springs all human misery.

Thus we spoke long round the subject. If we could not reach understanding through words, yet our silences were illuminating. Before a decision is taken our minds consult like doctors round a sick-bed. One is for using the knife, another wishes to spare the patient, and the third searches for a rare remedy. But of what avail are human councils and human wishes when disaster is written in the stars? Yet even on the eve of lost battles council of war is held.

The Prince and Braquemart planned to explore the pasture-lands that same night, and since they would not accept our guidance or escort we recommended old Belovar to them. Then we accompanied both to the foot of the marble stairway. We took formal leave of them, as one does when the meeting has been without warmth and fruitless into the bargain. Yet as epilogue there came an unspoken scene to confound me. The pair halted on the cliffs in the first pale light, scanning us long and silently. Already the cool air of the morning was rising, in which things are revealed to the eye as if they were unfolding, new and mysterious, in their first birth. So, too, the Prince and Braquemart as they stood. It seemed to me that Braquemart had lost his air of mocking superiority and was smiling humanly. The young Prince, for his part, had straightened himself and looked at us with a cheerful mien, as if he knew the key to the problem that vexed us. The silence lasted long; then Brother Otho grasped the Prince's hand once more and bent low over it.

After they had disappeared from sight over the crest of the cliffs I sought once more, before I went to rest, the gold-striped lily of Zipangu. Insect wings had already stripped the delicate stamens and the depths of the green-gold cup were flecked with purple dust. Doubtless the great night moths had scattered it in their nuptial flight.

So from each hour there flows mixed joy and bitterness. And as I bent over the bedewed blossom there rang out from the fringe of the distant forests the first cuckoo calls.

21

We spent the morning with unquiet minds, the abandoned vehicle still before our door. At breakfast Lampusa delivered to us a note from Phyllobius from which we learned that the visit had not escaped his notice. In it he asked us to give the Prince an urgent invitation to the cloister; Lampusa's tardiness in delivering it was disastrous.

At midday came old Belovar to inform us that the young Prince had appeared at his farm along with Braquemart at crack of dawn. There Braquemart, studying an illuminated parchment the while, had sought information on various localities in the forest. Then they had set off again, and the old man had sent out scouts from his clan on their trail. The two had vanished into the woods in the stretch between the Flayer's Copse and the Coppice of the Red Steer.

The news told us that evil was in the wind, and we would rather that they had set off with the henchmen and sons of Belovar, as had been proposed to them. We knew Braquemart's fundamental principle that none inspires more fear than the lone fighter, and considered it possible that they would seek out the man of blood amidst the splendour of his court and confront him face to face. But it came about that they fell into the nets of the powers of evil; we had a suspicion that Lampusa's tardiness had some connexion with the web. We thought of the fate of Fortunio, who had yet been a man of great gifts and had long studied the forests before penetrating into them. Doubtless it was his map which had come into Braquemart's possession by devious ways. After Fortunio's death we had searched for it long, and learned that it had fallen into the hands of treasure-hunters.

Thus the two of them had ventured into danger without preparation and without any ideal to guide them, as if it were some common adventure. They went like half-men — on the one hand Braquemart, the pure technician of power who saw only fragments and never the roots of things; and on the other hand the Prince Sunmyra, the noble spirit, who knew the nature of justice and order, but was like a child venturing into forests where the wolves are howling. Yet it seemed possible to us that Father Lampros could have altered them both deeply and made them whole men, as can happen with the aid of mysteries. We wrote him a letter telling him how things stood, and sent Erio off in haste to the cloister of Our Lady of the Crescent.

Since the appearance of the Prince and Braquemart at the Hermitage we felt anxious at heart, and yet we saw things more clearly than before. We felt that they were reaching their climax, and that we would have to swim for it as if caught in the broken waters of a gorge. We considered, too, that the time had come to keep Nigromontanus's mirror ready, and wished to light the flame by its means while the sun was still favourable. We climbed up on to the balcony and kindled the lamp in the prescribed manner, catching the fire from the skies in the crystal disc. With great joy we saw the blue flame descend, and hid mirror and lamp in the niche which holds the household gods.

We had not yet changed our garb when Erio returned with the monk's reply. He had found the Father in prayer; without reading our letter, he had handed the boy a written message. Thus are orders delivered which have long been sealed and ready.

We saw that for the first time the missive was signed with Lampros; in addition it bore the crest with the motto 'I bide my time.' For the first time, too, it made no mention of plants; instead, the Father requested me in brief terms to find the Prince and take him into my care. He added that I ought not to go unarmed.

Then it was a case of arming in haste, and, exchanging a few hasty words with Brother Otho, I drew on the old and well-tried hunting jacket which no thorn could pierce. It must be confessed that in the Hermitage we were ill-furnished with weapons. There was nothing but a gun such as is used for duck-hunting, but with a shortened barrel. We had used it at times on our journeys to shoot at reptiles, which combine a thick hide and a tenacious grip on life, and which coarse shot dispatched more surely than the best-aimed rifle. When my glance rested on it, memory called up for me the musky odour which the wind in the hot riverside thickets bore down to the hunter as he approached the spots where the great saurians leave the water. For those hours when land and water merge in the dusk we had set a silver bead on the barrel. This was the only thing in our house which we could call a weapon; I therefore took it down, and Brother Otho hung round me the capacious leather wallet with, on its flap, nooses for shot birds and sewn inside a belt for cartridges.

So in our haste we seize whatever first comes to hand; besides, it was likely that Father Lampros had recommended me to arm as a symbol of freedom and hostility, just as one comes bearing flowers in friendship. The good sword which I had worn with the Purple Horse hung in the North in my father's house; but for such an expedition I would never have chosen it. It had flashed in the sun in the heat of cavalry engagements when the earth thunders under the hoof-beats and the breast swells gloriously. I had drawn it during the swaying gallop forward when the weapons clash, lightly at first and then with growing volume, while the eye is already picking out the opponent in the enemy squadron. I had relied upon it, too, in those moments of single combat when one traverses the broad plain at the gallop in the midst of the mêlée, and empty saddles are already to be seen. Then many a blow was struck which fell on the guard of Frankish rapiers or the basket-hilt of Scottish claymores, and many too at which the wrist felt the soft resistance of naked flesh as the blade cut its mortal way. But all these, and even the free sons of the barbarian peoples, were men of honour who opposed their breasts to the steel for the sake of their native land; and at a feast one could have raised the glass to them like brothers. The brave of this earth determine in combat the boundaries of liberty, and weapons drawn on their like cannot be borne against executioners and their underlings.

In haste I took leave of Brother Otho and of Erio too. I interpreted it as a good omen that as I did so the boy looked at me with joyful assurance. Then I set out on my way with the old herdsman.

22

Dawn was already breaking when we reached the big farm-stead among the pastures. Even from a distance we saw that the place was in an uproar; the byres gleamed in the light of torches and resounded with the lowing of cattle being driven in with haste. We met a body of armed herdsmen, and learned that others were off in distant regions of the Campagna where there were herds to be hidden away. In the courtyard Sombor welcomed us, the old man's eldest son, a giant with a full red beard and in his hand a whip of which the tails were hung with leaden pellets. He reported that about noon a commotion had arisen in the woods; they had seen smoke rising and heard noises. Then from the marshy scrub which lined the Flayer's Copse there had advanced troops of 'glow-worms' and huntsmen who had driven off a herd grazing there in a distant pasture. It is true that Sombor had won back part of their booty before they had re-crossed the marsh, but in so doing he had identified groups of foresters, so that a sortie could be expected at any time. In the meantime his trackers had spotted patrols and single scouts at other points as well – at the Copse of the Red Steer and even in our rear. Good fortune had brought us to the farm just before we were cut off from it.

Such being the case, I could not expect old Belovar to accompany me on my thrust forward into the woods, and thought he would do well to look to his possessions and his folk. But I still misjudged the old warrior and the zeal he could show for his friends. At once he swore an oath that house and byre and barn might burn to the ground before he would allow me to take even a step alone that day, and transferred to Sombor the care of the farm. At these words the women-folk, who were already dragging the things of value from the house, quickly touched wood and thronged round us with wails. Then the old grandmother came up and laid her hands upon us from head to foot. On my right shoulder her fingers were arrested, but the second time glided over unchecked. But when she touched her son's forehead a fit of terror seized her and she covered her face. Then his young wife threw herself on his breast with the shrill lamenting wail that is the keening cry.

But Belovar was not the man to be moved by women's tears, least of all when the intoxication of battle ran in his blood. He cleared a space around himself with both arms, like a swimmer parting the waves, and with a loud voice called his sons and retainers to the fight by name. He chose only a patrol, leaving all the others to his son Sombor for the defence of the farmstead. But he picked none but those who had killed their man in the clan feuds, and whom he called his cockerels when he was in good humour. They came in leather doublets and leather hoods with the rude weapons which have been stored in the armouries of the prairie farms since the times of distant ancestors. There in the gleam of the torches were to be seen halberds and spiked maces and massive poles which bore keen axe-heads and saw-edged blades – pikes, too, scaling irons, and all manner of barbed hooks. So armed, the old man proposed to scour the woods of miscreants and sweep them away, as he had longed to do in his heart.

Then the kennel boys pushed open the doors behind which the packs barked and bayed, the slim coursers and the heavy mastiffs distinguished by their high- or low-pitched note. With lolling tongues and a deep growl they poured out to fill the courtyard, at their head the massive bloodhound, Leontodon. He bounded up to Belovar and, whining, set his paws on his shoulders, although the old man was a giant. The boys let them drink their fill, pouring blood for them to lick over the flags from a dripping bowl.

The two packs were the old man's pride, and he owed it to them without a doubt that the rabble from the forest villages had in the last years gone out of their way to avoid his farm. For his light pack he had bred the swift wind-hound of the steppe with which the free Arab shares his couch and whose young his wife suckles from her own breasts. In the frames of these greyhounds each muscle could be traced as if an anatomist had laid it bare, and they were so full of movement that even in their dreams a constant twitching ran over their bodies. Of all the fleet beasts of this earth, only the cheetah could outstrip them, and that only over a short distance. They hunted the game in pairs, cutting across its twists and turns; then they fastened on its shoulders. But there were also whippets that worked alone, which brought their victim down by the throat and held it till the hunter came.

In his heavy pack the old man bred the Molossan hound, a splendid fawn beast brindled with black. The intrepidity which marks this race was further strengthened by crossing the breed with the Tibetan mastiff, which used to be set against aurochs and lions in the Roman arenas. This strain showed itself in the size, the proud carriage and the tail, which they carried like a standard. Almost all these mastiffs bore in their hides deep scars – mementoes of blows from great paws during the bear-hunt. The giant bear had to hug the edge of the wood when it broke from cover into the pasture-land, for when the dogs on his trail had overtaken him and brought him to bay the mastiffs tore him to shreds even before the hunters could deal the final blow.

The inner court was filled with bounding dogs that growled and snarled as they licked their chops, and from the red maws we saw that gleam of their terrible fangs. To this was added the crackling of the torches, the clatter of weapons, and the lament of the women who fluttered here and there like startled pigeons. This was a din in which the old man revelled; with his right hand he stroked his beard complacently, while the left made his broad dirk dance in the red cloth girdle. He bore, too, a double-headed axe slung from his wrist by a leather thong.

Then the kennel boys rushed on the dogs with leather gauntlets reaching to their shoulders and coupled them securely with coral-red leashes. Then we passed through the gate with dowsed torches, and so over the farthest bounds of the pasture-lands towards the forest.

The moon had risen, and in its light I gave myself up to the thoughts which steal upon us when we go forward into the unknown. Memories rose up of wonderful morning hours when we rode with the advance guard in front of our columns, and behind us in the cool of the early day there resounded the chorus of the young horsemen. Then we felt our hearts beat so joyfully that all the treasures of this earth would have seemed dross to us compared to the imminent joy of sharp-fought and honourable action. Oh, what a difference there was between those moments and this night in which I saw glitter weapons like the talons and horns of terrible monsters. We were entering the Lemur-peopled woods where human justice and man-made laws are unknown; in them there was no fame to be won. And I felt the vanity of shining deeds and of honour – felt, too, great bitterness of heart.

Yet it was a comfort to me that I had not come under the spell of a mystical adventure as I had the first time when I sought Fortunio, but in a good cause and summoned by lofty spiritual powers. And I resolved not to give way to fear nor yet to overweening confidence.

23

While still in the neighbourhood of the farm we divided up our forces for the advance. We sent scouts ahead and had the coupled coursing hounds follow them, while the main-guard brought up the rear with the heavy pack. The moon-light had grown so bright that one could read the written word by its rays; therefore so long as we still marched across the pastures the individual detachments were easily kept in sight. On our left, too, we saw the three tall poplars like black lances, and in front the dark mass of the Flayer's Copse, so that we kept to our line of march without difficulty. We were advancing towards the curved sweep of wood where the sickle of the Flayer's Copse thrust forward from the high forest.

My place was at the side of the old fighter of blood feuds with the light pack, and from that position we kept the vanguard within sight. When it reached the girdle of reed and elders which bounded the swamp we saw them stop dead, then they pushed forward through a gap. Scarcely had they vanished from our view than we heard an evil, grating, snapping sound, which seemed to come from iron jaws, and with it a mortal cry. The scouts pushed back out of the brushwood into the open as we hastened forward to catch up with them and discover what was amiss.

We found the gap through which the scouts had passed knee-high in broom and heather. It glinted in the moonlight, and in its midst presented to our eyes a scene of horror. We saw hanging there like a trapped animal one of the young retainers, caught in the massive iron grip of a machine. His feet scarcely touched the ground, and head and arms hung down behind him among the undergrowth. We hastened up to him and saw that he had been caught in a woodcock spring – as the Ranger called the heavy mantraps which he had concealed where men would pass. The sharp edge of the jaw had severed his breast, and a glance sufficed to show that aid was impossible. Yet with joint effort we tensed the spring to free the corpse from the grip. When so doing we discovered that the trap was armed with sharp teeth of blue steel like the jaws of a shark. Once we had laid out the corpse on the heath, we carefully closed the jaws again.

It was naturally to be assumed that spies were keeping a watch on the trap, and indeed, as we still stood in silence round the dead victim of the villainous weapon, we heard a rustling in the scrub nearby and then a burst of loud mocking laughter in the night. Now a stir ran through the swamp as if a flock of crows had been disturbed from the sleeping perches. There was a breaking of branches and a scuffling in the gravel patches, and a rustle ran along the dark ditches beside which the Ranger had his hides for hunting duck. At the same time the marsh resounded with whistles and raucous voices, as if it were infested with a swarm of rats. We heard the rabble taking heart, as it does in the slime of the gutters and the hulks if it is sure that numbers are on its side. And, indeed, they appeared to be greatly superior to us in strength, for near and far we caught the ribald songs of the rogues' guilds. Thus hard by us the band of La Picousière roared their song. They stamped their feet in the marshy ground and croaked like frogs:

> Catherine a le craque moisi,
> Des seins pendants,
> Des pieds de cochon,
> La faridondaine.

And out of the high broom, the reedy thickets and the bushy willows the loud refrain echoed back. In this confusion we saw wild-fires dance on the stagnant waters, and waterfowl skimmed past on startled wings.

Meantime the main body with the heavy pack had also come up in haste, and we noticed that the retainers came near to wavering before this weird crowd. Then it was old Belovar who raised his voice in a mighty shout: 'Forward, lads, forward! The rabble is giving ground. Watch for the traps.'

With these words he began to push forward without a glance to right or left, making the blades of his double axe glint in the moonlight. Then the retainers too followed, burning to come to grips with the setters of snares. In little clumps we forced our way through reed and bush and tested the ground as best we might. In this way we looked for the passages between ponds on whose dark mirror the water-lilies gleamed, and slipped through the brittle bulrushes, scattering the cotton from their dark tufts. Soon we heard the voices close at hand and felt the whistle of the balls as they passed our temples. Now it was the turn of the kennel boys to excite the dogs until their coats bristled and their eyes sparkled like glowing coals. Then they were let slip, and with a whine of joy shot like pale arrows through the dark undergrowth.

The old man had been right in maintaining that the rogues would not stand and fight; scarcely had the dogs begun to bay than we heard plaintive cries which fled and were lost among the brushwood, and behind them the pack in full tongue, hot on the scent. We doubled forward after them and saw that beyond the brush there was a peat moor where the ground was level as a threshing-floor. Across this level space the rabble had taken flight and were racing for their lives towards the thick wood. But only those could win it who had not a coursing hound on their heels. We saw many who had been set upon by the dogs and had to turn at bay; like pale flames licking round the damned, the dogs surrounded them and sprang greedily at their throats. Here and there, too, the fugitives had been brought down and lay on the ground as if hamstrung, for a single dog held each one by the neck.

Now the boys let slip the heavy pack, and with a howl the mastiffs rushed forward into the night. We saw them leap upon their victims and bring them down; then, fighting over it, they tore their prey apart and scattered it in fragments on the ground. The kennel boys followed and gave the *coup de grâce*. This was a scene from hell devoid of mercy. They stooped over the dead and threw the dogs their reward. Then, with greater effort than before, they leashed the hounds anew.

So we stood upon the moor on the threshold of the dark forest. Old Belovar was in good humour, praised man and dog for their work and distributed brandy. Then he pressed on to a new advance before the forest was put into alarm by the fleeing rabble, and had a breach laid bare with hatchets in the thick-set hedge which bounded it. We were not far from the spot where I had penetrated with Brother Otho to find the red woodland orchid, and it was Köppels-Bleek we planned to attack first.

Soon the breach was as wide as a barn door. We kindled torches and entered the high forest through the dark jaws.

24

Like red pillars, the trunks gleamed in the light of the flaring torches; their smoke rose perpendicularly in fine thread-like wisps which, high above our heads, wove a canopy in the unstirred air. We moved forward in extended order, bunching to force our way past fallen trunks and then spreading out again. But by the aid of the torches we kept each other well in sight. To ensure that we did not lose the path the old herdsman had brought sacks filled with chalk, and with it had a gleaming white trail laid. So he ensured our line of retreat.

The hounds advanced on Köppels-Bleek, drawn as ever by the scent of evil and the shambles. Under their guidance we gained ground rapidly and moved gradually to the head of the column. Only now and again a bird flitted down with a beat of heavy wings from its nest in the tree-tops. And silently swarms of bats circled in the glow of the torches.

Soon I seemed to recognize the hill on the edge of the clearing; it was lit by the dull reflection of glowing fire. We halted, and heard once again the sound of voices carried over to us, but they had lost the braggart note they had before up on the moor. It seemed that here detachments of foresters had taken up position to defend the woods, and Belovar proposed to sweep them aside as he had already done with the outlaw bands. He brought the coursers to the van and lined them up as if for a race; then he sent them into the darkness like glowing shot. As they tore their way through the bushes we heard opposite us whistles and then howls, as if they had come up against the wild huntsman himself. They had clashed with the bloodhound pack which the Chief Ranger kept in his kennels.

Of these savage mastiffs, their ferocity and strength, Fortunio had told me things that bordered on legend. In them the Chief Ranger had carried on the stock of the Cuban mastiff, which is red-haired and has a black mask. Long ago the Spaniards had trained these dogs to tear Indians to shreds, and had exported them to all lands where slaves and overseers are to be found. With their aid the Negroes of Jamaica had been subjected again after they had assured their victorious rising by force of arms. Their appearance is described as terrifying, for hardly had the slave-hunters landed with the coupled hounds than the rebels, who had held fire and steel in contempt, offered their submission. The leader of the red pack was Chiffon Rouge, a beast dear to the Chief Ranger, because he was in a direct line by birth from the bloodhound Becerillo, whose name is linked in such a sinister manner with the conquest of Cuba. It is reported that his master, Capitano Jago de Senazda, set him to bait captured Indian women as a spectacle to entertain his guests. Thus in human history there ever recur moments in which it threatens to come under the sway of Satan.

From the terrifying cries we knew that our light pack was already lost before we could even send help. It was doomed to be exterminated all the faster since it was of pedigree stock, which fights to the death instead of giving ground. We heard the red couples after their first baying close in to grapple; as their howling died away and their jaws met greedily on flesh and fur, the clear bark of the windhounds whimpered into silence.

Old Belovar, who had seen his noble beasts sacrificed in the twinkling of an eye, began to storm and curse, and yet he dared not throw in the Molossan hounds after them, for they were our strongest remaining card in the uncertain game. Therefore he called to his retainers to look to their arms; then they rubbed the breasts and jowls of the great beasts with spirit of henbane and fastened round their necks spiked collars to protect them. The others set the torches in dead branches in preparation for the fight.

All this took but a moment, and scarcely had we taken up position than the red pack burst upon us like a storm. We heard them break through the dark bushes; then the beasts leapt round the circle within which the torchlight lay like the glow of fire. At the head was Chiffon Rouge, round whose neck there sparkled a fan of knife-sharp blades. He held his head low and let his tongue loll dripping to the ground; the eyes blinked and peered out from under his brows. From a distance one saw the bared fangs glisten, with the lower pair protruding over the lips like tusks. In spite of its weight, the huge beast sprang forward with light bounds – with little dancing gambols and leaps aside as if in its overpowering strength it disdained to attack us in full career. And behind him there appeared the bloodhound pack, black and red in the light of the torches.

At the sight cries of fear rang out and there rose loud calls for the Molossan hounds. I saw old Belovar glance anxiously at his mastiffs, but the proud beasts, with sharp eyes fixed ahead and pricked ears, pulled on the leash undaunted. Then the old man laughed to me and gave the signal; as if shot from a taut bowstring, the yellow hounds flew upon the red pack. At their head Leontodon rushed upon Chiffon Rouge.

Then under the massive trunks in the red light there was a howling and triumphant baying as if the legions of hell were charging past, and the lust for death spread on all sides. In dark masses the animals rolled and worried at each other on the ground, while others on the heels of the enemy raced round our position in a wide circle. We attempted to intervene in the fray, which filled the air with its clamour, but it was difficult to pick out the red hounds with spear or shot without injuring the Molossan dogs. Only where hunter and hunted circled us in their race was it possible to take aim at individual dogs and bring them down like wildfowl. Here it became evident that in my weapon I had unwittingly made the best possible choice of weapons. I attempted to fire when my eye saw the silver sight cover the black mask, and was then certain that my shot would bring down the beast and halt it in full career.

But over on the other side, too, we saw the flash of shots, and guessed that from there they were shooting down the Molossan dogs in their tracks. Thus the skirmish was like a hunt which formed an ellipse round two points of fire, with the heavy pack fighting on the shorter axis. In the course of the fight the track of the hounds was lit by columns of fire, for where the torches fell to the ground the dry brushwood flared up into a blaze.

Soon it was obvious that the Molossan dog was superior to bloodhound, if not in strength of jaw, then certainly in weight and power of attack. But the red dogs were superior in numbers. It seemed, too, that from the other side still more fresh couples were being thrown into the fray, for we found it more and more difficult to give support to our hounds. The bloodhounds had been carefully trained to attack human beings, whom the Chief Ranger held to be the best of game; and when the Molossan dogs were no longer in sufficient numbers fears for our own safety distracted our eyes from the hunt. Now from the shadowy bushes, now from the thick smoke of the fires, one of the red beasts would hurtle upon us, and its approach was heralded by cries. Then we had to look to it in haste that it was shot down in its charge; yet many were halted only on the pikes of the retainers, and on many a one the double axe of Belovar whistled down when it already lay upon its victim, thirsting for blood.

By now we could see the first ill-omened signs of cracking in our ranks; it seemed to me, too, as if the cries of the retainers were louder and more anxious; in such situations an undertone of quiet weeping tells us that despair is threatening to draw near. With these cries there were mixed the howling of the packs, the report of the shots and the crackling of the flames. Then we heard resounding from out of the thickest wood a mighty peal of laughter, a roared guffaw, which intimated to us that the Chief Ranger was taking part in the action. In this laughter there rang out the fearful joviality which marked his character; he still had something of the great lord who exults with joy when challenged to the fight. And then fear was his element.

In this confusion I began to get hot, and felt that excitement was gaining the upper hand in me. But, as often before in such situations, there rose in my mind the picture of my old master of fence, van Kerkhoven. The latter, a little Fleming with a red beard, who had trained me in footwork, used often to say that an aimed shot is better than ten fired at random. He impressed upon me, too, that at the point in the battle when panic threatened to spread I should hold out my extended index finger and breathe calmly. For he was the strongest who had drawn a good breath.

Kerkhoven, then, sprang to my mind; for all true teaching is a thing of the spirit, and when we are hard pressed the spirits of good masters stand by our sides. And as I had done once upon a time in the North on the shooting range, I halted to draw a long, deep breath, and felt my sight grow clearer and my breast less constricted.

Most dangerous of all, as the battle turned against us, was that the thick smoke more and more limited our field of fire. Thus the fighters became isolated and objects lost their definition. Then, too, the red dogs burst out at ever shorter range. Therefore more than once I saw Chiffon Rouge cross the front of my position, but whenever I attempted to take aim the cunning beast made for cover. Then the hunter's lust to kill and the passionate desire to lay low the Chief Ranger's favourite bloodhound tempted me to leap after it the next time I saw it disappear into the thick smoke, which flowed past me like a broad stream.

25

Now and again in the thick smoke I thought I saw the shadowy form of the monster, but always too fleetingly for a well-aimed shot. Besides, phantasms in the coiling wreaths deceived me, so that in the end I halted in my uncertainty and stood listening. Then I heard a crackling of twigs, and the suspicion seized me that the beast might have cast about to attack me from the rear. To protect myself I knelt down with raised rifle and chose a thorn bush to cover my back.

It often happens in such situations that our eye is caught by trivial objects, and so on the spot where I knelt I saw a plant blossoming among the dead leaves and recognized in it the little red woodland orchid. I must therefore be on the spot which I had reached with Brother Otho, and consequently hard-by the eminence near Köppels-Bleek. And so it was; with a few steps I gained the little crest which rose like an island from the smoke.

From the ridge I saw the clearing at Köppels-Bleek shimmer in a dull glow, but my gaze was diverted far into the depths of the forests to where a great fire raged. There I saw rising in flames – tiny and seemingly fashioned from red filigree – a turreted and towered castle. I then called to mind that on Fortunio's map this spot was marked 'Southern Residence'. The fiery glow revealed to me that the attack by the prince and Braquemart must have penetrated as far as the steps of the palace; and as always when we see the results of gallant deeds, a feeling of joy rose in my breast. But simultaneously I recalled the triumphant laughter of the Chief Ranger, and hastily I turned my eyes on Köppels-Bleek. There I saw things which in their infamy made me grow pale.

The fires which lit Köppels-Bleek still glowed, but a white layer of ashes covered them with silver domes. Their glimmer fell on the flaying-hut, which stood wide open, and coloured the grinning skull on the gable with red light.

From footsteps on the earth around the fires and signs in

the cavernous interior, which I will not describe, one could see that the Lemurs had celebrated here one of their loathsome festivals, and its afterglow still lay over the spot. We human beings look on such deeds of darkness with bated breath and catch but a glimpse of them.

It suffices to say that among all the old and long since fleshless heads my eye caught sight of two new ones hoisted high on poles – the heads of the Prince and of Braquemart. From the iron pike-heads with their curving hooks they looked down upon the glow of the fires which were flaking away to ash. The young Prince's hair had turned white, yet I found in his features greater nobility and the lofty, sublime beauty to which only sorrow gives birth.

At the sight I felt tears start to my eyes, but they were such tears as fill us with wonderful exultation together with their sorrow. On this pale mask from which the scalped flesh hung in ribbons and which looked on the fires from the elevation of the torturer's pike there played the shadow of a smile intensely sweet and joyful, and I knew that on this day the weaknesses had fallen from this noble man with each step of his martyrdom, like the rags of a king disguised in beggar's weeds. Then a shudder ran through my inmost heart, for I realized that he had been worthy of his forefathers, the tamers of monsters; he had slain the dragon fear in his own breast. Then I was certain of something which I had often doubted – there were still noble beings amongst us in whose hearts lived unshakeable knowledge of a lofty ordered life. And since a high example leads us in its train, I took an oath before this head that from that day forth I would rather fall with the free men than go in triumph among the slaves.

Braquemart's features, on the other hand, looked quite unchanged. He glanced down on Köppels-Bleek from his pike with irony and a faint air of disgust; his feigned tranquillity was that of a man who feels a violent internal conflict, but allows no sign to show in his countenance. It would therefore hardly have surprised me to notice in his eye the monocle he wore in life. His hair, too, was still black and glossy, and I guessed that he had taken in time the pill which every Mauretanian carries on his body. It is a capsule of coloured glass, generally carried in a ring, or, in moments of peril, in the mouth. A bite suffices to crush the capsule, in which is sealed a poison of rare potency. This is the procedure which is described in the language of the Mauretanians as the appeal in the third instance; it corresponds to the third degree of violence and fits the concept of human dignity they cherish in this Order. They consider that it is impaired by anyone who suffers violence with indignities; and they expect of each Mauretanian that he should be prepared for death's summons at any hour. Such, then, was the last adventure of Braquemart.

I looked at the sight numbed with horror, and without knowing how long I remained before it, as if I were outside of time. At the same time I fell into a half-dream in which I forgot the nearness of danger. In such a state we pass like sleep-walkers through perils, not picking our way, but close to the spirit of things. So I stepped on to the clearing at Köppels-Bleek, and things were distinct, as in drunkenness, but not external to me. They were as familiar as in a child's fairyland, and round about the pale skulls on the old trees regarded me questioningly. I heard shots, too, whistling across the clearing – the deep hum of the heavy crossbow bolts and the sharp report of the muskets. They passed so close that the hair was stirred on my temples, but I heeded them only as a deep melody which accompanied me and gave the measure for my steps.

So in the shine of the silvery fires I came to the seat of terror and lowered the pike which bore the Prince's head. With both hands I raised it from its iron spike and laid it in my leather wallet. As I knelt and finished the task I felt a sharp blow on the shoulder. One of the shots must have found its mark, yet I felt no pain, nor did I see blood on my leather jerkin. But my right arm hung useless. As if awaking from sleep, I looked around me, and hastened back into the wood with my precious trophy. My musket I had left where we found the orchid; in any case it would

103

serve me no more. Therefore I made all haste to reach the spot where I had left the fighters.

Here it had become completely still, and even the torches flickered no more. Only where the bushes had flared there still lay a shimmer of red glowing ash. By its light the eye could distinguish on the dark ground the corpses of fighters and dead dogs; they were mutilated and horribly mauled. In their midst against the trunk of an old oak lay Belovar. His skull was cleft and the gushing blood had dyed his white beard. The double-headed axe at his side and the broad falchion, which his right hand still gripped firmly, were blood-red too. At his feet was stretched his trusty Leontodon, its skin torn to shreds by shot and steel, and, dying, it licked his hand. The old man had fought well, for round him lay mown a ring of men and dogs. So he had found a fitting death in the heat and din of the chase in which are woven death and sensual pleasure. For long I looked into the eyes of my dead friend, and with my left hand laid a handful of earth upon his breast. The Great Mother whose wild, tumultuous festivals he had celebrated is proud of such sons.

26

To find my way out of the deep forest on to the pasture-lands I had only to follow the trail we had blazed on our advance, and, deep in thought, I walked along the white path.

It seemed strange to me that during the fight my place had been with the dead, and I seized upon it as a symbol. Then, too, I was still under the spell of a dream. This condition was not entirely new to me; I had experienced it earlier in the evening hours of days when death had passed me by. At such times the activity of our minds causes us to be detached a little from our bodies and we move about like an escort at the side of our own image. But up till now I had never felt these fine ties so loosened as here in the wood. As I dreamingly traced the white trail, the world appeared like an ebony forest in which there gleamed little ivory figures. In this way I traversed the marsh beside the Flayer's Copse and came out on to the Campagna not far from the tall poplars.

Here I saw with alarm that the sky was ominously lit with the glow of fires. On the pasture-lands, too, there was a sinister hurrying to and fro, and shadows hastened past me. Perhaps amongst them there were retainers who had escaped from the fight; but I refrained from hailing them, for many seemed in a drunken rage. I saw some, too, brandishing torches, and heard the argot of La Picousière's men. Bodies of them laden with booty were already hastening back to the woods. The Coppice of the Red Steer was brightly lit: there the cries of women mingled with the laughter of a triumphal feast.

Full of evil foreboding, I hastened to the prairie farm, and even from afar could not but see that by now even Sombor and his men had fallen to the rabble. The rich steading was bright with flames, which had already unroofed house and barn and byre, and the 'glow-worms' danced howling in the firelight. Looting was in full swing; they had already cut open the beds and filled them like sacks with booty. Other groups I saw carousing with the contents of larder and cellar. They had staved in the tops of casks and drew their liquor with their hats.

The murderers were at the height of their debauch, and this fact favoured me, for I passed half-sleeping through their midst. Dazzled by the fire, by killing and with drunkenness, they moved like the animals one sees at the bottom of troubled pools. They passed close by me, and one who bore a felt cap full of brandy raised it towards me with both hands and stumbled off cursing when I refused his toast. Thus I made my way through them untouched, as if I had the *vis calcandi supra scorpiones*.

When I had left the ruins of the farmstead I noticed something which increased my alarm still more, for it seemed to me that the glow of fires was paling in my rear; but not so much because of the distance as because of a new and more terrible red which mounted in the sky before me. Even this part of the pasture-lands was not without movement. I saw, for instance, scattered cattle and herdsmen in flight, and, above all, in the distance my ear caught the baying of the red pack, which seemed to be drawing near. So I hastened my steps, although my heart was filled with fear at the terrifying rings of fire which I was approaching. Already I could see the Marble Cliffs rising darkly like sharp reefs in a sea of lava. Still hearing the hounds at my back, I clambered up the steep crest from the edge of which our eyes had so often drunk in the beauty of this earth and felt its exaltation; now I saw it under the pall of ruin.

Now the extent of the destruction could be read in towering flames, and far and wide the old and lovely towns along the Marina stood bright in ruin. They sparkled in fire like a chain of rubies, and from the dark depths of the waters there rose their shimmering image. The villages and farms, too, burned throughout the land, and from the proud castles and the cloisters in the valley the fires shot up. The flames towered smokelessly like golden palms into the unstirred air, and from their crowns there fell a golden rain of fire. High above this whirl of sparks, touched with red light, flocks of doves and herons which had risen from the reeds soared in the night. They circled until their plumage was enveloped in flames; then they sank like flares into the blaze.

Not a sound mounted up to me, as if all space were devoid of air; the spectacle unfolded in terrible silence. Below me I could hear neither the children weeping nor the mothers wailing, nor the war-cry of the clans nor the bellowing of the cattle in their byres. Of all the terrors of destruction, only the shimmering golden light of the flames rose up to the Marble Cliffs. So distant worlds flared up to delight our eyes in the beauty of their ruin.

Nor did I hear the cry which issued from my mouth. Only deep within me, as if I myself were engulfed in flames, did I hear the crackling of this blazing world. And it was only this gentle crackling that came to my ear as the palaces fell in ruins and from the harbour store-houses the cornsacks flew high into the air to scatter their glowing contents. Splitting the earth, the powder magazine at the Cock Gate blew up. The heavy bell, which had graced the belfry for a thousand years and had accompanied countless persons with its tolling in life and death, began to glow, darkly at first, and then with increasing brightness; finally it crashed from its bearings, wrecking the tower in its fall. I saw, too, the pediments of the pillared temples gleam in the red rays, and from their lofty pedestals the images of the gods with shield and spear bowed down, to sink without a sound into the raging flames.

Before this sea of fire I was seized for the second time, and more strongly than before, by the dreamlike trance. And since in that state our senses catch many things at once, I heard, too, the pack drawing incessantly nearer, with the rabble at its heels. Already the hounds had almost reached the foot of the cliffs, and in the pauses I caught the deep bay of Chiffon Rouge with his pack howling behind him. But in my state I was unable to stir a foot, and I felt my cry halt on my lips. Only when the beasts were already climbing into view did I manage to stir; but the spell remained. So it seemed as if I floated gently down the marble stairway, and with a light spring I cleared the hedge which enclosed the Rue-Garden Hermitage. And behind me in a tight-packed troop the savage chase rushed jostling down the narrow cliff path.

27

In my leap I fell on the soft earth of the lily-bed, and I saw with amazement that the garden was wonderfully illuminated. The flowers and bushes gleamed in the blue radiance as if they had been painted on porcelain and brought to life by a charm.

Up in the court before the kitchen stood Lampusa and Erio, intent upon the blazing fires. Brother Otho, too, I saw in holiday garb on the balcony of the Hermitage; listening intently, he was looking in the direction of the rock stairway down which the rabble and the hounds broke like a torrent. Already they had rushed along the hedge in a swarm and fists were drumming on the garden gate. Then I saw Brother Otho smile as he raised and scrutinized the rock-crystal lamp, on which there danced a small blue flame. He seemed hardly to notice that meanwhile the door had burst under the blows of the hunters and that the sombre pack had broken triumphantly into the lily-beds, at its head Chiffon Rouge with the blades sparkling round his neck.

In my distress, I raised my voice to call Brother Otho, whom I saw still standing and listening on the balcony. But he seemed not to hear me, for he turned with unmoved gaze and, carrying the lamp before him, entered the herbarium. So I then called to Lampusa, who stood before the entrance to the rock-kitchen, her face lit by the glow of the fires, and I saw her, with her arms crossed and a grim smile baring her tooth, glance fleetingly into the tumbling mass. Then I knew that from her no pity could be expected. So long as I got her daughters with child and struck down my foe with the sword I was welcome; but to her any conqueror was a son-in-law just as a man in straits was an object of contempt.

Then, as Chiffon Rouge gathered himself to spring, it was Erio who came to my aid. The boy had seized the silver quaich which still stood in the courtyard after the offering to the snakes. He struck it, not as of wont with his pearwood spoon, but with an iron fork. Thus he sounded on the bowl a note which was like a peal of laughter, and halted man and beast where they stood. I felt a stir in the clefts beneath the foot of the Marble Cliffs, and then a fine piping, repeated a hundredfold, filled the air. Through the blue radiance there shone a bright gleam, and like lightning flashes the lance-head vipers shot from their crevices. They glided through the beds like pale whipcords, and from under their coiling lashes there rose a whirl of petals. Then, forming a golden circle on the ground, they raised themselves to man's height. In this posture they swayed their heads like slow-beating pendulums, and their fangs, bared for the attack, had a deadly gleam like lancets of curved glass. Accompanying this dance, a gentle hissing like iron cooling in water pierced the air, and from the beds a fine clatter of horn arose like the castanets of Moorish dancers.

Within the circle of this dance the rabble stood as if turned to stone, and their eyes started from their sockets. Tallest of all rose the Griffon; with her bright shield she swayed before Chiffon Rouge, and as if in play encircled him with the figures of her twining rhythms. The monster followed the swaying of her undulating dance, trembling and with bristling coat; then the Griffon seemed to graze him gently beside the ear, and, shaken by the cramps of death, with bitten tongue, the bloodhound rolled in agony among the lilies.

That was the sign for the dancers, who threw themselves on their victims in golden coils so closely interwoven that men and dogs seemed to be enveloped by a single scaly body. And it seemed as if only a single death-cry rose from this elastic web, and that the subtle choking power of the poison stifled at once. Then the glinting braids unwound and the snakes glided gently back to their clefts.

Standing among the beds which were now strewn with dark corpses swollen with poison, I raised my eyes to Erio. I saw the child enter the kitchen with Lampusa, who was carrying him with a mixture of pride and tenderness, and with a smile he waved back to me as the creaking rock door shut behind him. Then I felt my blood flow more freely in my veins, and sensed that the spell which had seized me was broken. Once again I could move my right hand freely, and in haste I entered the Hermitage, for I had fears for Brother Otho.

Traversing the library, I found the books and manuscripts laid out in perfect order, as one arranges them when going on a long journey. The round table in the hall bore the images of the household gods – they were well furnished with flowers, wine and offerings of food. This room, too, was festively decorated and glowingly lit by tall tapers of the knight Deodat. In it I felt myself as much at home as I found it bravely decked.

While I was thus gazing at his work, Brother Otho appeared above from the herbarium, leaving its doors wide open behind him. We fell into one another's arms and related our several adventures, as we had used to do in lulls in battle. When I recounted how I had come upon the young Prince and drew my trophy from the leather wallet, I saw Brother Otho's features grow hard; then with the tears a wonderful radiance spread over his face. We washed the head clean from blood and the sweat of death with the wine that stood beside the food-offering; then we laid it in one of the great scent amphorae in which there withered the petals of white lilies and roses of Shiraz.

Now Brother Otho filled two goblets with the old wine, and, having poured the libation, we emptied them and broke them in fragments on the hearthstone. Thus we celebrated our departure from the Rue-Garden Hermitage and with sorrow left the house which had become a warm shelter for our spiritual life and brotherly companionship. But we must quit every spot which has given us haven on this earth.

So, forsaking our possessions, we hastened through the garden door towards the harbour. I held the amphora in both arms, and Brother Otho had the mirror and the light safely against his breast. When we reached the bend where the path loses itself in the hills towards the cloister of Our Lady of the Crescent, we halted once again and looked back to our house. We saw it lying in the shadow of the Marble

Cliffs with its white walls and the broad slated roof on which the shimmer of distant fires was dully mirrored. Like dark ribbons, the terrace and the balcony wound round the light walls. That is how they build in the pleasant valleys where our people have set their dwellings on the southward slope.

As we looked at the Rue-Garden Hermitage its windows lit up, and from the gable a flame sprang aloft to the highest edge of the Marble Cliffs. In colour it was like the tiny flame in the lamp of Nigromontanus – a deep dark blue – and its tip was jagged like the cup of the gentian. Thus we saw the harvest of many years of labour fall a prey to the elements, and with the house our work sank into the dust. But on this earth we may not count on seeing our work brought to completion, and he must be held fortunate whose resolve survives the struggle without inflicting on him too much pain. No house is built, no plan laid, of which decay is not the corner-stone, and what lives eternally in us does not lie in our works. This we perceived in the flames, and yet there was joy in their radiance. So we hastened along the path with fresh strength. It was still dark, yet from the vine-yard terraces and river meadows the morning cool already rose. Our hearts felt that the fires in the sky had begun to lose something of their balefulness; they were mingled with the red of dawn.

On the slope of the hill we saw the cloister of Our Lady of the Crescent also enveloped in glowing fire. The flames licked up the tower so that the golden horn of plenty, which swung upon the spire as weathercock, shone bright. The high church window on the side of the imaged altar was already burst, and in the empty space we saw Father Lampros stand. At his back it glowed like the mouth of a furnace, and in order to hail him we hastened forward up to the cloister graves. He stood there in his festal robes, and on his face we saw a bright and unfamiliar smile, as if the fixed expression which had used to frighten us in him had melted with the fire. He seemed to be listening, and yet he did not hear our calls. Then I lifted the Prince's head from the scent

111

amphora and raised it high with outstretched arm. When we saw it we shuddered, for the moisture of the wine had drawn the rose petals so that the head now seemed lit with dark purple splendour.

But it was yet another sight that held our gaze as I raised the head – we saw the still undamaged circle of the rose window fill with green light, and its pattern was strangely familiar. It seemed to us as if the image had gleamed for us once before in the plantain Father Lampros had shown us in the cloister garden; so the secret symbolism of the spectacle was revealed.

As I stretched the head towards him, the Father turned his eyes upon us, and slowly raised his hand as at the consecration of the Host, half in greeting and half pointing; on it the great cornelian glowed in the fire. As if with this gesture he had given a sign of terrifying power, we saw the rose window disintegrate in golden sparks, and, with the arch, tower and horn of plenty collapsed upon him in mountainous ruin.

29

The Cock Gate had fallen in; we forced a way over its ruins. The streets were strewn with fragments of walls and beams, and round about in the embers lay scattered corpses. We saw terrible scenes in the cold smoke, and yet a new confidence had come to life in us. Thus the morning brings good council, and the mere return of the light seemed wonderful to us after the long night.

In this scene of devastation the old feuds seemed as senseless as memories of a debauch. Nothing but misery had remained, and the combatants had laid aside their banners and insignia. We still saw plundering forest bands in the sidestreets, but by now the mercenaries were taking up position in pairs. At the Barbican we met Biedenhorn, who was posting them and assuming an air of great importance.

He stood in the square in his golden cuirass, but without his helmet, boasting that he had already decorated Christmas trees – that is, he had seized the first that came to hand and strung them up on the elms on the town wall. In accordance with military tradition, he had stayed well entrenched during the disorders; now that the whole town lay in ruins he emerged to play the man of destiny. Beyond that he had a good grasp of the situation, because on the round tower of the Barbican there already waved the banner of the Chief Ranger, the red boar's head.

It seemed that Biedenhorn had been drinking deep; we found him in the grim good-humour which made him the darling of his mercenaries. He was filled with undisguised delight that it went hard with the writers, versifiers and philosophers of the Marina. As well as the odour of creation, he hated wine and its wit-sharpening qualities. He loved the heavy beer they brew in Britain and the Netherlands, and considered the people of the Marina snail-eaters. So he was a man of hard blows and hard drinking, and believed unshakeably that any scruple on this earth can be overcome by a good pommelling. In this respect he had something in common with Braquemart, but he was sounder to this extent, that he despised theory. We had a regard for him because of his good nature and good appetite, for, if he were unsuited for his post on the Marina, who can blame the wolf set to guard sheep?

By good fortune Biedenhorn was one of those men whose memory is stirred by a morning glass. Therefore we did not need to call to his mind the moment before the passes when he with his cuirassiers had been hard-pressed. There he had been brought down, and we saw the free peasants of Alta Plana already busy forcing open his coat of mail as if they were breaking the shell of a lobster at a banquet. By now the dirk was tickling at his throat; then we cleared a space around him and his men with our Purple Horse. It was during this sortie that young Ansgar fell into our hands. Then Biedenhorn knew us from our Mauretanian times, and so it came about that he required no pressing when we asked him for a ship. There is no gainsaying that the hour of catastrophe is the Mauretanian's hour. He placed at our disposal the brigantine which he held in the harbour, and detailed a group of mercenaries to accompany us as escort.

The streets leading to the harbour were packed with fleeing people. Yet it appeared that all did not wish to leave the city, for we saw the smoke of sacrifices already rising from the ruins of the temples and heard hymns rising from the wreckage of the churches. In the chapel of the Sagrada Familia, hardby the harbour, the organ had escaped undamaged, and its mighty chords accompanied the hymn the congregation sang:

> Princes are men of women born,
> And turn again to lowly dust;
> Their council's might is overborne,
> And in the grave their state is lost.
> Since no man then can give us aid,
> We turn to God in our great need.

At the harbour there was a press of people laden with the remains of their belongings. But the ships for Burgundy and Alta Plana were already overladen, and each skiff which the boatmen pushed off from the quay with their poles was followed by a loud cry of despair. Amidst all this misery Biedenhorn's brigantine – as if under a taboo – swayed at its mooring buoy, which was picked out in black, red and black. She shone with dark-blue varnish and copper fittings, and when I gave the order to push off the crew drew the covers from the red-leather cushions of the thwarts. While the soldiers kept the crowd at a distance with their pikes we succeeded in shipping some women and children, until our deck was only a handbreadth above water. Then the crew rowed out of the inner basin behind the harbour wall; beyond it a fresh wind caught us and drove us forward towards the mountains of Alta Plana.

The cool of the morning still lay over the waters, and the eddying winds drew cat's paws on the surface of its glassy green mirror. But the sun was already pushing up above the jagged peaks of the snow-covered mountains, and the Marble Cliffs rose gleaming out of the lowland mists. We looked back to them and let our hands trail in the water, which turned blue in the sunlight, as if the shadows had taken refuge in its depths.

The amphora we treasured carefully. We did not yet know the fate of this head which we bore with us, and which we delivered to the Christians when they raised the great cathedral on the Marina from its ruins. They buried it beneath the foundation stone. But before that day Brother Otho addressed to it an eburnum in the chapel of the Sunmyras's ancestral home.

30

The men of Alta Plana had moved up to the frontier when the glow of fires lit the sky. Therefore even before landing on the shore we saw young Ansgar, and he waved gaily to us.

We rested a little with his men while he sent a messenger to his father; then we mounted slowly to the farm in the valley. When we reached the passes we halted for a time at the great Tomb of the Heroes and before many another of the small monuments that stand there upon the battlefield. In so doing we came to the narrow pass where we had cut a way for Biedenhorn and his men. At this spot Ansgar gave us his hand anew and said that from now on of all his possessions half was ours.

At midday we caught sight of the farmstead in the shelter of its oak grove. On seeing it we felt that we had come home, for, as in the north of our land, we found united under the shelter of its broad roof barns, stables and house. The door was wide open and the sun danced on the threshing-floor. The cattle looked down upon it over their feeding-racks, wearing today upon their horns trinkets of gold. The great hall was decked for a holiday, and from out of the circle of men and women awaiting us stepped old Ansgar to bid us welcome.

Then we passed through the wide open door as if into the haven of our father's house.

MORE ABOUT PENGUINS
AND PELICANS

For further information about books available from
Penguins please write to Dept EP, Penguin Books Ltd,
Harmondsworth, Middlesex UB7 0DA.

In the U.S.A.: For a complete list of books available
from Penguins in the United States write to Dept DG,
Penguin Books, 299 Murray Hill Parkway, East
Rutherford, New Jersey 07073.

In Canada: For a complete list of books available from
Penguins in Canada write to Penguin Books Canada Ltd,
2801 John Street, Markham, Ontario L3R 1B4.

In Australia: For a complete list of books available from
Penguins in Australia write to the Marketing Department,
Penguin Books Australia Ltd, P.O. Box 257, Ringwood,
Victoria 3134.

In New Zealand: For a complete list of books available
from Penguins in New Zealand write to the Marketing
Department, Penguin Books (N.Z.) Ltd, P.O. Box 4019,
Auckland 10.